The Zombie Interviews

Wolf Larsen

Please note: This work can either be read as a book, or performed as a play. Either way, I do not give permission for the text of this book to be changed in any way, regardless if it is performed on stage, or if it is published again in a later edition.

Another note: I do with grammar & spelling & capitalization as I choose. As far as the Queen's English goes, the Queen can give me a blow job! (If she pays my rent.)

ABOUT WOLF LARSEN

Wolf Larsen is a comedian, writer, and poet who has traveled through over 50 countries. Wolf worked for years as a seasonal laborer in Alaska. His fiction and poetry has been published in literary magazines around the world.

Other Books by Wolf Larsen

Capitalism Sucks (non-fiction)

Honky Fucking Crazy N-Word Lover (a novel)

Pricks, Cunts, & Motherfuckers: The Novel About New York City

Eulogy for the Human Race (poems)

Pornography (poems)

Penis! Penis!! Penis!!! (a play)

Ten Thousand Penises in Your Ear (a novel)

There are many other books by Wolf Larsen to choose from. Most of Wolf's books can be purchased at online retailers.

The Zombie Interviews

By Wolf Larsen

How to Fix World War 3 With a Wrench

The Reader Interviews Wolf Larsen

Reader: Do you Jump out of spaceships? Do you Eat yourself now & then?

Wolf: Only when I Get snorted up somebody's nose, then people confuse me with cocaine! You see, sometimes the music Screams so much Crashing Europe at me! But other times, So many streets haunted with Loneliness. And then, there's the Dripping minutes of the day Haunting me with time! Knife stabbings! Octopuses! Toilet paper! And that's why I Love it when people feed me to the ducks!

Reader: But what about your Sexual affair with a run-on sentence, back when you were Living inside of that painting by Edward Münch?

Wolf: Scandal! Artillery! Clogged toilets! Watch out for walls melting! The Violent verbs & angry adjectives are coming! And that's why I Don't have a pair of buttocks anymore! No, wait! That's wrong! That's right! What was the question?

Reader: Nevermind! Tell us about the Years you lived in a cardboard box on the sidewalk!

Wolf: Oh, that! Used condoms! Empty beer cans! Solitude! But you see, Fresh feces be talking to you! And then there's Aircraft carriers that sometimes show up in your toilet. There was the time that I Was attacked by this Foreign navy

8

floating in my toilet. And then there was the time that I Was swallowed by a black hole in outer space!

Reader: And what about All the cum of strangers?

Wolf: That's Jesus Christ on a hamburger! Or maybe it's the Virgin Mary with calamari! And then there's always Talking to yourself for hours on end. Used toilet paper! Saturn's rings! Vomit!

Reader: In your past, you were swallowed by empty spaces that went on for years. And then there was the time that you impersonated the Second coming of Christ, and nearly started a nuclear war. Looking back on all of that, how do you feel about Having sex with my dog, the four-legged one?

Wolf: Well, you see, I would jump off a tall building with a condom, because you have to have protection. And that's why you can't Walk down the street naked if you're the President! But you can Start a nuclear war if you're President! And that's why I Stick my tongue up God's ass. And I believe in bLow jobs! Of course, most people believe in Getting blow jobs from tooth fairies. But I think that's a bunch of Flying saucers!

Reader: That's very interesting! But what about That time that you were dancing naked on the bus going downtown?

Wolf: What about it?! You see, Monkeys really are smarter than humans! And anyway, I always Paint my orgasms all over God's face in endless bright colors! (Except when I Have to pee.) But that's only on holidays, the Holidays of

Masturbation. Because on normal days I Like to have sex with other people's dogs, the four-legged ones. On abnormal days I Might abduct your children, and eat them. And every night I Masturbate to the sounds of lunacy coming from Washington DC. Except when I Can't find my right hand.

Reader: But you never Walk in the sunlight! Is that true?

Wolf: It's completely true, and it's completely false! It's completely true because I lost my penis on the subway train. But it's completely false because of all the Gargoyles in the dungeon butt-fucking the Priest. But really, the truth has something to do with bunny rabbits & doggy testicles. Or maybe it has something to do with the fires of Hades burning all the empires down. And then there's always Anal sex with God to consider.

Reader: Many of your fans love your S&M fetishes. And your enemies hate you, Because of all the exotic civilizations growing out of your head. Of course, many of your fans are your enemies. But what about the Time you had sex with a homeless person in an alleyway?

Wolf: Well that's very Catholic with the sexy Italian priest whipping & whipping me! And it's also very Blueberry with lots of Charles Manson! But when you consider the Wonderful ecstasy of whipping & whipping, and you consider the Ceilings of all the world painted with Your fantasies, then it's Crashing church bells for everybody! Because it's obvious that words Are dripping in our heads like cum! Especially on days when Flying

12

gargoyles be crashing into Western civilization! (The Testicles of Aristotle hold the true knowledge.)

Reader: Sometimes, when you're dAnCiNg-iN-cAnCeR, people think you are really A different species from a different planet. Do you care to address that?

Wolf: Testicles! Poison! Sweetness! And that's why I have athlete's foot in my butt! Especially with All these female orgasms flying around! Because when I'm Traveling in heroin vacationland, I'm really a bunch of fluid colors! I hope that clarifies the issue with Why I collect used tampons going back for thousands of years. But, there's also some Pipe-smoking of bizarre adjectives involved. Or maybe I lost my virginity to a Monster in your imagination. Or maybe The sunshine is smiling at me!

Reader: And then there's the Hope of Castration. Some people think you're a porn star pretending to be the Catholic Pope. Is that true?

Wolf: It's true if Elvis Pressley is alive somewhere! But then there's always Transsexual Ballerinas to consider. Especially with all the Sunshine Going wild! But I'm really Very very Catholic even though I don't believe in God. I'm so excited about the Immaculate conception between my right hand & my penis every day! Especially on Yesterday-kind-of-days! But then, because of my childhood of Stealing people's heads and playing basketball with them, then Let's party! This probably has something to do with my Enormous pubic hairs! But I love

all the Psychiatric Temples of Wife
Swapping! I absolutely do!

Reader: But that's so Pumpkin pie! It's
also a pecan-bazooka-Hieronymus-
Bosch-with-a-big-Dick-kind-of-music!
What do you say to that?!

Wolf: What do I say to that? I say that
Donkeys running for political office are
Asses! Asses! Asses! Asses! And then
there's the Elephants always licking
Satan's balls! And of course, there's lots
of War to eat at the Bakery of
Impossibilities! That's why I always Wipe
my ass with Donkey politics! You see?

Reader: No, I don't see! You can't Have
sex with a computer, if the biG-
cOmPuTeR-Dick isn't Blessed by a monk!
Right?

Wolf: Wrong! I always said, 'Touch your penis before you shake a politician's hand', and that's why Armadillos! It's also why Masturbating on a subway train while everybody else watches is a bubblegum delight! You see, Big buttocks of 500 pound women are really sexy in Spandex! And then there's the Police. And that's why I always Give the police a urine sample in their open mouths. And something else I always say, is 'You better stick your own finger up your own butthole before you Paint a Picasso'.

Reader: But that's only true if Lots of oranges! Have you thought about that?

Wolf: Have I thought about it? That's all I think about! No, that's not true! Everything is true! Because Purple-Crazy-Yesses taste great with Adjectives! And then there's the Museum of What's

Crazy Today. And sometimes, You just have to search for yourself in a public toilet.

Reader: But, time is made out of Everything. And to be the Devil's advocate, Jumping off a cliff won't make you any taller. What do you say to that?

Wolf: Zombies! Tits! Excitement? But, Hordes of Happy alcoholics are not the answer! Or are they? And lots of Anorexia Sprinkled everywhere! And really, if you think about it, Everyone is Their own special kind of Spicy sauce! And sometimes, Everyone is Having a giant party inside Her vagina. But, there's always exceptions. Like when People think themselves into A maze of Happy diseases of the mind. Or when the Storms of everyone else are looking for you. So there's all that to consider.

Reader: But When we reach our hands into each other's butt Holes, we discover The meaning of life. Isn't that true?

Wolf: Only if Crazy-crazy-crazy goes out for a walk. And that there is the Talking buttholes! But you have to be careful about Getting lost in somebody else's butthole, particularly if their butthole is really really big! And nobody's really sure about Space aliens getting lost in the Statue of Liberty's vagina. Of course, Our own anuses are the birthplaces of space aliens! But sometimes I Crash my car into some fairytale. And other times I Hijack somebody else's brain for a day or so. It's all Nobel Prize committee with lots of urine-smelling-alleyways!

Reader: I see. But what about Making your doo-doo right in the middle of the United Nations?

Wolf: Well, actually, lions & tigers in your balls is really Great! And Skyscrapers of syphilis growing out of your skin! It's the reason that The streets keep running away from here. But only on Tuesdays. And the fireworks of Up the booty! It's why the Palaces of Procreation are popping up everywhere! And then there's the Highways that suddenly rush you off to your past. But it's all balanced out by the Helicopters in the sky crashing into the Words on this page. Sniffing glue with all the monkeys in the zoo is especially true! Especially when All the street corners are floating away! Salvador Dali's Balzac may come to haunt us one day. And that's why we need to Take a shit right now!

Reader: Point well taken! After all, So many fish swimming around your

thoughts. But what do you say about
Having sex with your mother?

Wolf: I say that It's all lots of Tornadoes!
Except when You order The Daily Special
from a cannibalistic butcher. I also think
Human bodies hanging from the ceiling
of a butcher shop makes my mouth
water. But I don't think that either!
Actually, I think that Fish jumping out of
question marks and eating you is
wonderful. And Rocket blasts of classical
music is so overwhelming! It's absolutely
alcoholic Streams of wonder flowing by!
Even on Centuries Of LSD that last until
Tomorrow! For example, last Friday I
Jumped out of A book and surprised the
passerby on the street! But sometimes
that also happens on Mondays. But
Mondays is usually when Dozens of
ghosts float out of my Past, and haunt
me for a century. Avalanches of Crack-

cocaine rocks is something especially to be careful about! You never know if All your dead relatives will show up for dinner. Especially after an avalanche of Crack-cocaine rocks!

Reader: I see. But what about Your mother? She's really sexy, isn't she?

Wolf: That's why we need S&M bondage! S&M bondage is the reason for Politics! And S&M bondage is why we Are as happy as squirming worms! Otherwise, Lots of nuclear submarines would happen. And that's why we need Haunted houses 365-days-a-year.

Reader: Well, that's Zigzagged! It's been really A giant fantasy talking to you. I hope to have you on the show again sometime.

Wolf: Yes! Thank you! And thank you for the Syphilis!

Biting My Own Ass

A Neanderthal Interviewing a Dude on
the Bus

The Neanderthal: Why you no Bite my
ass? How come All the orgasmic verbs
taste so Rainbow? What Hallucinations
on toast have you come to give me?

Dude-on-the-Bus: A thousand virgin
ladies with strap-ons are coming to greet
you! Too much Ceiling above me! Now!
Lots of Sunshine in my crack-cocaine!
Human blood splashing everywhere, you
see! And that's why Cannibalistic-cow-
patties! cAnNiBaLisTiC-cOw-pAtTieS!
CaNnIbaLiStiC-coW-paTtiEs! Now, waltz

around this ballroom with a mass
murderer! You gotta mass murder before
you Sit on the toilet! That's why I always
paint my childhood with Catholic priest
jism! Can't you see the lions & tigers in
my eyes? And so much Honesty To give!
Too much Psychedelic psychiatry To
give!

The Neanderthal: If too much
Psychedelic psychiatry To give, then why
Do you smear your face everywhere?

Dude-on-the-Bus: Because you gotta Eat
the boogers of all your friends & family,
before you Can jizz your hallelujah
everywhere! You gotta Feed wild drugs
to your dogs & cats, before you Join the
army of zombies! You gotta Make war
with All the imaginary people! Especially
before you Play that music of murder!
Serenade! Artillery! Masturbation!

The Neanderthal: That don't make no Sense, unless you put lots of Nonsense on top of it! Why you Exploring the Music with your penis?

Dude-on-the-Bus: Because Of All the wild staircases of philosophy leading Us into The big toilet in the sky! Learn from the penis wisdom of Monsters! Even if I Sometimes blast a planet full of people into pieces, I still Care! And even if I Play chess with Prehistoric man, then I still Care about Ping-Pong-balls & pInG-pOng-baLLs & piNg-poNg-BallS! Can't you see? Can't you see the Russian roulette Of caring? You must see the Russian roulette Of caring! Otherwise, you won't see the Hordes of Horny words Headed your way! Even a Rabidgrowling-dog knows that Sidewalks can lead to Heaven!

The Neanderthal: That some Confusion with lots of bullets flying everywhere! Everybody knows Knife stabbings are Kisses from God! So why don't you Get married?

Dude-on-the-Bus: What? What Round-and-round are you asking me? I am the Charles Manson of the Animal kingdom! And I am the Nuclear Prophet of the Subway station! Even the Rats in the subway know that I'm the Santa Claus of their wet dreams! So you gotta be Generous with Your sperm, if you're gonna be King of the Rainbows! You gotta see the Manifestations of Glorious gods masturbating everywhere! Gunshots?

The Neanderthal: Exactly! That's exactly what I'm Conspiring about! Thank you for that Morse code full of nipples! But what about the Syphilis monsters Tiptoeing everywhere?

Dude-on-the-Bus: I'm not Running around naked about that! I'm not even Doing drive-by shootings about that! You see what I'm about, I'm about the Buttholes that want to be filled with nuclear missiles! And I'm about the Peace pipes of crack-cocaine being passed along on the subway train! I don't give no Nuclear war about the Syphilis monsters!

The Neanderthal: Well, don't you think that sometimes you gotta Eat a politician's ass to Discover nirvana?

Dude-on-the-Bus: Say what? What kinda Greasy hamburger is that? You gotta have Lots of pussy eating, to be the Prince of Pussy! You got to be the Prince of Pussy, to hear the Dogs howling in your balls! And you gotta hear the Dogs howling in your balls! You gotta Be the conqueror Of the clouds! And you gotta be able to Quack-quack the Duck between your legs, if you want to Party with the Wild Neanderthals of Manhattan!

The Neanderthal: What does that have to do with Fucking your mother?

Dude-on-the-Bus: That has everything to do with Fucking my mother! It's all about the Fucking Of your mother! You can't Be a transvestite preacher of Mass murder, if you don't Have a Cock of Steel! And you can't Fuck this sentence. So Fly away into Your mother's vagina! Even the Angels in my semen know that!

The Neanderthal: Are you sure? Are you sure that the Angels in your semen know that?

Dude-on-the-Bus: Yeah, because I got castrated! And if My castrated penis don't sing, then you know that The world be Fucked up! And You know that The world be As Fucked up As the world be fucked up. So then you know that Satan's butthole loves you! And if Satan's butthole loves you, then you know that The sun will shine. The sun will shine until All the big booties of the world fart us some new philosophy!

The Neanderthal: I stand corrected then. But what about the Lakes of Insanity? What about the Butthole of God swallowing Everything?

Dude-on-the-Bus: That's not even Up as a flying cloud! It's not even As Down as a dandelion growing out of a corpse's head! It's so ding-a-Ling with lots of Everybody! Everything is so Fiery with Music burning everywhere! That's why I get drunk off of Musical notes! You see?

The Neanderthal: I see. But then there's the Fungus of Joy growing all over us. What about that? And what about the Millions of psychopaths swimming up our fallopian tubes? And what about the Misery of All the smiling people in the photos? And how about the Children that are eating the Stars in the night sky?

Dude-on-the-Bus: Nuclear war!

The Neanderthal: That's it? That's all?

Dude-on-the-Bus: That's it!

Why Your Mother is so Horny!

An interview with an Orangutan at the zoo

A pig on the farm: So, how's the Hundreds of psychopaths living in your home?

The orangutan at the zoo: What? Mass murder?

The pig: I mean, All the voices in the heads of the hundreds of psychopaths living in your home! How's the crazy zoo of domestic life going?

The orangutan: Not now! Too much Blue sky In the crackhouse we're living in! Hot pickles! Herpes? Why am I Sucking on the tit of a Crack whore? Why am I always Jumping off a cliff? What's So scrambled in my thoughts? You know it's wrong With So much Righteousness?!

The pig: That's so Orgasmic! So How was your Orgasmic trip to Heaven?

The orangutan: Cockroaches! Now! Now the Giant cockroaches dance to the waltz! Yes! No to the Orangutans of Mars in bed with my wife! Butthole! So much Raspberry buttholes with whipped cream! You Should try the Queen's vagina!

The pig: Me? But what about your Overflowing Sewage brains?

The orangutan: That's a thousand dead men hanging from a tree! Burning yesterdays! Wow to the Holes in the sky! Scissors to the Scrotums of Jupiter! Night sky to the Van Gogh canvases of neurosis!

The pig: Night sky to the Van Gogh canvases of neurosis? But that's so Nursery school with toddlers running amok with chainsaws! What's the Prognosis?

The orangutan: It's Society collapsing into a bunch of diarrhea! Siamese twins! Herpes! Herpes to the Circus elephants! Circus elephants to The Chimpanzees! Subway trains! Subway trains to Yesterday! That's why I Gave my eyes away! And tomorrow! Lots of tomorrow!

The pig: Lots of tomorrow? Lots of tomorrow?? Lots of tomorrow???

The orangutan: Lots of tomorrow with lots of Lunacy! Lots of Lunacy with lots of Chocolate! And lots of Chocolate with lots of Blue sky! And now! And yesterday! And outer space! With lots of Blood!

The pig: Don't you think all that Happiness is causing all the mass riots?

The orangutan: No, because of the Total eclipse of the Butt! Yes, because of Igor Stravinsky attacking the solar system with his music! And maybe, because of the Verbs they send us to eat through our minds! You have to see Alcoholism as the Gift of the Crazy monkeys crawling all over the Clouds! But seeing What everybody else Doesn't see is The Gift of the Artist. Because the artist be hopping around Like a Grasshopper! With lots of LSD rainbows everywhere! Always! Lots of LSD rainbows everywhere!

The pig: Some people would say that's Hypocritical with lots of Pigs in the mud.

How do you respond to that? Do you Cry
yourself to sleep with a rifle in your
hands?

The orangutan: I love pork! I Masturbate
my jism all over my barn animals! Yes! I
Conquer with lots of Human meat
barbecues! But! Yes! Only after I've been
chased across the Imagination of Jesus
Christ by crack-smoking leopards &
coyotes! Mustard!

The pig: But mustard all over Your words
is so mEnTaLLy-iLL-piE! Don't you think
so? And don't you think the Polar bears
in Hawaii will be offended?

The orangutan: I think! Yes! I think! I
think & I think & I think! I think All the
vibrators & dildos of the world will attack
any moment now! I think We're going to
be swallowed by So many languages that
don't exist yet! And I think Traffic lights

are totally Sexy! But sometimes no I think! But when I no think, Then The gates of Leprosy opens, and I forget which universe I'm in! With lots of! Yes! Toilets! Boogers!

The pig: Boogers? Boogers? Boogers?

The orangutan: Yes to boogers! Yes to booty holes! Yes to scratching your balls! 24 hours a day ball scratching! 24-hour-ball-scratching will save humanity from The philosophies of talking grasshoppers! And 24-hour-ball-scratching is great for The King of Hemorrhoids!

The pig: Ball scratching! Ball scratching! Ball scratching!

The orangutan: How's Your wife's pregnancy from the neighbor's German Shepherd going? What's the Yes doing making love to the no? When is the

World going to break down? Why is the Universe going Berserk with you? You answer! Me you answer!

The pig: I no answer, Because Lots of piranhas in my underwear! I yes answer, because Slow Spreading of the Poetry disease!

The orangutan: That's exactly what I'm talking about! I'm talking about Burning down the sky! I'm talking about Feeding death to the Living! I'm talking about Monsters in everybody's Happiness!

The pig: Can you please shoot me?

The orangutan: Yes.

(He pulls out a gun and shoots him.)

The Intersection of Heaven & Hell

A Hallucination interviews a prison
inmate in solitary confinement

A hallucination: So what if We all Go to
work Naked Today?

The prisoner: Exactly! That's So Artificial
intelligence in the 13th century! It's so
Flying oranges in the 13th century that
it's Gangrene! What Collapsing Sky!
What Exciting Toads & frogs to talk to!

The hallucination: So what about Frying
up some Of the passerby To eat? Do you
think the Avalanche of People will Taste
delicious?

The prisoner: Yes! Because pornography
Tastes delicious with religion & feminism!

And that's why I love to eat feminists & priests! Yippee! Somersaults! You Eat me now! And that's why the planet Earth wants to be devoured by my favorite frog! It's the mystery of Words on fire!

The hallucination: The mystery of Words on fire? And The roller coaster of Everything be spinning & jumping & flying around you! So what Spicy Human flesh are we going to eat today?

The prisoner: That's Very spicy! It's practically Verbs doing the naughty-naughty-naughty in the bedroom! You must Unhook yourself from The planet Earth! I must Become a new species! We must all Become a new species! Eat Buildings! And then you will understand the highways to Other imaginations! Jumping off a mountain of Impossibilities is the way! That's the way to the salvation of Genital warts! That's why Fireflies speak so much pornography!

The hallucination: But what Pornographic Civilization? And whatever the Lickety lips licking the passing clouds? Can you jump and jump and jump so far away?

The prisoner: The magical mushroom philosophy of Mentally-ill-space-aliens is here! The cRaCk-cOcAiNe-cApiTaLiSm of mentally-ill-store-manikins is there! The Neuroses of smiling misery is everywhere! Watch out! Watch out for the Torpedoes of Lust! The priests of the underworld are invading! So much invasions! Invasions of Insanity! Invasions of Colors everywhere! Invasions of Mass orgies across the nation! That's why I protect myself with a thousand brightly-colored dildos hanging from my body!

The hallucination: You protect yourself with a thousand brightly-colored dildos hanging from your body? Aren't you afraid of the Legions of Mentally ill rampaging through the streets?

The prisoner: I'm more afraid of the Penis of God! And then, there's the Dirty tenement streets singing to me! The Privilege Of poverty is everywhere! Have lots of Spermatozoa ready for everybody! 'Specially with Words attacking each other in broad daylight!

The hallucination: You Drinking that Ancient history Again? And you Smoking that Futurism Again? And you Murdering with Your mouth Again?

The prisoner: There's too many Birds flying between my ears! Too many Psychopaths crawling all over the darkness! So much sHaKiNg-pLaNeT-eaRth*!*

The hallucination: Lots of sHaKiNg-pLaNeT-eaRth? Or, lots of Magic talking to you from all the doorways Of your imagination?

The prisoner: It's horizontal! It's diagonal! It's Out-of-this-Sanity! Tomorrow is Coming with lots of Bazooka craziness!

The hallucination: Tomorrow is Bazooka craziness?

The prisoner: Tomorrow will never exist! That's why every tomorrow I Jump off the roof of a 100 story building! Apricots! Peaches!

The hallucination: Apricots? Peaches? The Princess of In-&-Out is doing the iMpOsSibLe-&-poSsiBle with her vibrator

Again, and all you can say is Apricots &
Peaches?

The prisoner: Bubblegum! That's the
reason for skipping butt naked through
the trenches of some war! So much
bubblegum! And That's the reason for
Earthquakes! So much hemorrhoids for
breakfast! And That's the reason for Your
eyeballs falling out!

The hallucination: But Siamese twins is
the reason for playing Russian roulette
with your mother, isn't that true? And is
it true that the continents of Europe &
North America be crashing against each
other again & again?

The prisoner: The continents be crashing
against each other?! But what about
Fairies-with-wings with their AK-47s
doing peace & love? And what about the

Explosions of Delirium always attacking reality??

The hallucination: No, that's On some other planet! It's lots & lots of worms crawling through the words, isn't it?

The prisoner: Isn't it Faraway? Or is it So close that all the insanities can see you? The volcano of everything! I have the happiness of nothing! So Giant octopuses holding machine guns in each one of their 10 tentacles! So pink breasts with Schoenburg! That's Saturday night with Razor blades! It's Flying saucers with Polish sausage! You Dating?

The hallucination: Yes! It's fabulously Yesterday with strawberry shortcake on top! It's extravagantly Hopeless! No music to cure my hemorrhoids?

The prisoner: No apples for Monsters!

44

Everybody Has An STD

A cat on a plate interviews the man
that's eating him

The cat asks as it's being eaten: You
fighting all the Penises in the sky with
your pet scissors?! And what about The
Extraterrestrial hiding in your closet? And
how come Your daughter got pregnant
from the German Shepherd?

The man eating the cat answers: Well,
that's all very Philosophical with runny
eggs! What we need to think about is the
Consequences of Breaking into people's
houses & shitting on their beds! And then
there's the Sexy lampposts dressed up in

French Lingerie! So we have to Be
flexible with the Wife swapping!

The cat: That's Fantastic with lots of
Pussy juices! A big fat woman Sitting on
Your face! Flying plates smashing
everywhere against the walls – how
come?

The man: Very Pumpkin pie with a
monster's erection! So Heavenly with
Lots of hell! Cactuses Up our asses now!
Massive-raging-Sex riots now! Herpes for
me now!

The cat: But Rabbits love you! Lots of
dead people with you? Too many
babbling Charles Manson clones in your
head? What spaghetti Is in your head?

The man: Spaghetti in my head? My
head is a racecar course of Crazy circles!
Race car course of Crazy circles in my

head! Race car course of Crazy circles in everybody's head! Big lips with lots of head! Lots of head with Big lips! Everybody has a Problem with their head! No?

The cat: Everything is no! Everything is Poisonous with Smiling rage! So Rabid Emotions with everything! No?

The man: No psYchO-maNic-hOmeLesS-pEopLe to eat today? No scRaMbLed-bRaiNs to Dance to? No museums of Contemporary art to shit in front of the paintings of?

The cat: Lots of Buttholes-full-of-cum with you, no?

The man: Lots of Buttholes-full-of-cum with me? What about the knives-jumping-out-of-the-eyes with everybody? Everybody no Fascinated with Buttholes-full-of-cum? That's why American apple pie with Buttholes-full-of-cum! American apple pie is why Anal Sex in heaven is so good! And why not?

The cat: Why not Shoot the Pages with eVeRyThiNg-iN-yOuR-iMaGiNaTioN? But what about the Music pounding out of all the peace & quiet?

The man: That's very Sometimes! It's also very Satanic Church! All your childhood memories are rumbling all around Somewhere! Your childhood is here! Your old age is here Too! It's lots of Knives slashing-out-of-these-words! Everywhere is Terminally ill!

The cat: Lots of Impossible people to that! And to that, I slice off my ears! So what about Blood on the walls? Do you think the Hamburgers of freedom will

Triumph over evil totalitarianism? Or will the Sunshine Spank all of us??

The man: Exactly! Yes! Lots of yes to Blood on the walls! Lots of exactly to Eating our own flesh! You know, Eating your own flesh is good for Rainbows. That's So groovy with lots of pubic hairs! Constantly-talking-gargoyles! So! Lollipops! Crabs in your pubic hairs to Talk With you with All day!

The cat: The whole Crabs-in-the-pubic-hairs thing is taking the nation by storm! So what's the Prognosis for discovering Poetry growing all over the universe?

The man: Well, there's the Lots of forever! And then there's the Oinking pigs that want to be eaten. And of course, always Oinking & more Oinking & more Oinking! Sometimes Nuclear war be Too many Mooing cows for my

Hemorrhoids! And now it's time to vomit the English alphabet everywhere!

The cat: But now is lots of Invaders from Your imagination Trampling all over us! And lots of Bananas in our butts, too! So how about the tarantulas Crawling up our butts?

The man: So, how the wife in the brothel doing? See how the Crazy penises go Swimming around the Circus! Especially, with so much machine guns spreading so much joy! Now I'm high on Zombie Meat! I look forward to Kissing baboons in zoos everywhere! Everybody looking forward to kissing baboons and kissing baboons and kissing baboons!

The cat: But with everybody looking forward to Kissing baboons, how will We go vacationing with all the Extraterrestrials?

The man: That's very 69 with cherry sauce on top! You have to look at the Canadian geese flying into Literary criticism! And what about All the monsters in your mental diseases?! And consider the Crashing cars throwing the musical notes all about! Everything considered, I think delicious cats are full of hope. So, Sodomize yourself with everything! Celebrate the presidential elections with So much pornography! Talk pornography with the Canadian geese!

The cat: Well, thank you for your Thousands of buttholes! I have to Shit some Bourgeois democracy now! And the audience has to Kill each other! So, Go paint some Liberty & justice all over the sheets when you jack off this afternoon!

The man: Very Car crashes in outer space! See you In heaven!

Everything You Needed to kNow about Sticking a Bottle in Your Butt

Your dog interviews a space alien

Your dog: What's Cooking in the Insane asylum?! You can't Have sex with an asteroid if You have to take a shit? Big hairy butthole! Right?

The space alien: Anal sex the sky now! I always said, 'Touch your penis so We all go Bonkers with Joy!' And that's why Mermaids taste like cat! It's also why Your Frankenstein penis is Precious! You see, Big buttocks of 500 pound women are really sexy with Science fiction. And then there's the Police. And that's why I always Give the police a urine sample in their open mouths. And something else I always say, is 'You better stick your own finger up your own butthole before you Sing at the opera.'

Your dog: But that's only true if You're having sex with Siamese twins at the zoo. Have you thought about that?

The space alien: Have I thought about it? That's all I think about! No, that's not true! Everything is true! Because Nobody really understands How big hairy buttholes swallow whole galaxies. And then there's the Schizophrenic food on your plate talking Mating rituals with your ears. And sometimes, You just need to hug a hungry grizzly bear.

Your dog: But, We clearly need more schizophrenic words to eat! And to be the Crazy man's advocate, What about

the Testicle spaceships of Salmonella?
What do you say to that?

The space alien: Chicken shit! Cancer!
Cancer? But, Fornicating rats in the walls
Don't understand me! And lots of
Philosophy to eat! And really, if you think
about it, Philosophy tastes like a man's
ass. And sometimes the philosophy Of
eating a man's ass Is Crazy-crazy
everywhere! But, there's always
exceptions. Like when an ant on the
ground swallows a human being. Or
when the desert winds are throwing
words at you. So there's all that dripping
pussy to consider!

Your dog: But a thousand gorillas All
masturbating on a space station
Together is very Butt-fucking-finger-
licking-good! Isn't that true?

The space alien: Only if Christopher
Columbus & his 3 ships are sailing up
your butt! And that there is the Answer
to a thousand gorrillas all masturbating
on a space station together. But you
have to be careful about Shoving glow-
in-the-dark vibrators & dildos up your
nose. And nobody's really sure about the
city neighborhoods moving back-&-forth.
Of course, Sticking a gun into your
Vagina is very sexy! But sometimes I
Vomit The Queen's English all over
myself. And other times I Grab my spear
and set out to attack My imagination. It's
all Hallways of Forever wandering
around!

Your dog: I see. But what about Space
aliens in the Bible?

The space alien: Well, actually, space
aliens in the Bible invented Banquets of

pussy eating! Space aliens in the Bible is the reason that Pussy tastes like the Apollo mission to the moon! And space aliens in the Bible is why My erection is 7 ½ inches long. And then there's the ducks swimming around the Porno movies. But it's all balanced out by the Battleships steaming out of the Buttholes of paradise. Boogers is especially true! Especially when The garden of Eden is in your butt! That's why Transvestite store manikins with huge penises may come to haunt us one day. And that's why we need to Be prepared with Whipped cream all over our naked bodies!

Your dog: Point well taken! After all, words be jumping! Plus, you have to Eat excitement all the time! But what do you say about the planet Earth being swallowed by a Chimpanzee's vagina?

The space alien: I say that this wonderful architecture of penises & vaginas is Very today! Except when yesterday hits you upside the head. I also think kangaroos jumping into my butt is Absolutely delicious! But I don't think that either! Actually, I think that it's a bunch of Bellybuttons, except when Jesus Christ serves you burger & fries at McDonald's. And Zombies in your pants is so overwhelming! It's absolutely Ketchup & mustard all over your Sexual fantasies! Even on Fridays! For example, last Friday the Apollo mission to the moon crashed into my wet dreams! But sometimes that also happens on Mondays. But Mondays is usually when the Armies of Dildos cum to Open your mind. Boobs bouncing all over the sky is something especially to be careful about! You never know if the continent of North America will just get up and walk away into outer space...

Your dog: I see. But what about the Orgies of All the species of the world fUcKinG-eaCh-oTheR-tOgeTheR?

The space alien: That's why we need hairy scrotums to save us! Gyrating horizons is the reason for jacking-off-in-the-morning and jacking-off-in-the-morning and jacking-off-in-the-morning! And mountains moving everywhere! This is why we Ride rocketships into the magical imaginations of other species throughout the universe. Otherwise, Art galleries in people's buttholes would happen. And that's why we need a police state with lots of jizz!

Your dog: Well, that's fascinating! It's been really musical talking to you. I hope to have you on the show again sometime.

The space alien: Yes! Thank you! And thank you for the dead person!

How to Drink Yourself to Death

The Pope in Rome interviews An
astronaut in outer space

The Pope: Why you no skip & hop all the
way to 1970s Manhattan? How come the
weather is So naughty with anal sex?
What dandelions talking to you all night
long?

The astronaut: It has something to do
with Drinking human blood, I think! Too
much collapsing Everything! Now! Lots of
naked-sexy-words running all over these
pages! Everything is itchy with music,
you see! And that's why you always feel
this banging-banging-banging inside!

Now, I was a Man with five heads once! That's why You gotta peel off your skin before you Scream out the seven forbidden words! And That's why I always deliberately crash into Mirages along the highway! Can't you see the words re-creating everything? And so much incest slobbering all over these walls! Too much verbs flying everywhere for me!

The Pope: So why the Exploding volcano of a face You giving me?

The astronaut: Because you gotta eat out the Virgin Mary's pussy before you Get to heaven! You gotta Lose the planet Earth before you Carve scientific equations all over your skin! You gotta get Around-the-clock before you Jump on Saturn's Rings and fly off to Nowhere! Mermaids! Whorehouses! Guns!

The Pope: That don't make no up-&-down! Why you eat my entire family?

The astronaut: Because I am the booty-eater to the Devil! I always give blow jobs to all the animals in the zoo! Even if I have 5,000 penises growing out of my crotch, I still love to Eat dead people! And even if I forget my mind back at the house, then I still Have an anus! Can't you see? Can't you see the pronouns searching for you? If you can't see the pronouns searching for you, then you won't see the Poetry frolicking all around you as you're walking down the street! Even a capitalist politician with his head stuck up his butt knows that Dandelions have supernatural powers!

The Pope: That Is some fried human brains with Sautéed onions! Everybody knows God is gay! So why don't you chop up the universe into pieces with that knife of yours?

The astronaut: What? What delirious Nincompoop are you asking me? I am the Toilet Sitter of the Babylons! And I am the Boomerang of the Butt worshipers! Even the ducks swimming on the moon know that I'm the King! I'm the King of Flying Outhouses! So you gotta be happy with your doo-doo, if you're gonna be Blueberry pie! You gotta see the elephants flying, to be Sure of Being swallowed by a happy cannibal! Marshmallows?

The Pope: Exactly! That's exactly what I'm upside-down about! Thank you for that car crash! But what about the murder in that smile?

The astronaut: That's why I Took a shit this morning.

40,000 Ejaculations

A Nun interviews a Porn actress

The nun: What you Going bananas about? And you know The Priests of Bubblegum religions? What Hooliganism today?

The porn actress: This Heroin Daydream! Huge phallus worship temples now or maybe! You see the Huge phallus temples? That's why God loves your booty hole! And about the Cyanide Cake, that's Martian bellybuttons to you! We gotta Connect to the Humanoids of the future, if they're not extinct yet!

The nun: How Sunshine is this? Which Phallus Temple is performing The magic Of Pooh-pooh this week? Is your butt Kosher with Futurism?

The porn actress: My butt is Kosher with Radio signals, which is so "Awoke" with Talking Diarrhea, and that's how We Dance with lions & tigers! This is Baboon wisdom kissing the Universe with Lots of WOW! The why is making love to the what! What Space aliens playing Russian roulette With vibrators is this? It's all a lot of pOrNoGraPhic-aRt-gRaFfiTi in sexy Colors! Of course not! It's what the On-fire-Skin is! And that is the Up doing lots of Coke With the around! Which is the Way out of this cRaZy-ciRcLe-oF-nOrMaLitY!

The nun: But Sexy feet has something to do with this, no?!

The Porn actress: But No & yes at the
same time! And that's the Drive-by
shooting of the matter! Now, lots of
Knives everywhere smiling at you! So
much Murder with your green eggs and
ham! And that's the Chainsaw massacre
that we so adore! So we need some!
Some chainsaw massacre on Christmas
so Divine! Or maybe some Wild animals
from the jungle high on cocaine!

Now about the Revolving-solar-systems
Of cocaine! Lots of circles! Erotic circles!
Erotic circles swinging around the Orgies
at City Hall! Or maybe Some Penises
with your beans & rice. Sometimes Our
faces be Silently spewing adjectives
everywhere. Lots of times Our faces
drool with so much anger & frustration,
that we lose our skin.

Watch out for the Bazookas of sex!
Incoming! Incoming Kangaroos with
landmines attached to their bodies!
Death! Lots of death with Sweetness!
And life too! Lots of life with Flying
bullets! It all balances out with Pink skin
drooling down the walls...

The nun: So! Which is what? That's The
question we must all answer with
Cunnilingus!

The porn actress: Cunnilingus is so
peanut butter that it should be one of the
10 Commandments! Exactly the yUmMy-
yuMmy-pRoTeiN we need!

The nun: But the Sexy mermaids
swimming around our apartments is so
cRacK-cOcaInE-sUnRisE! Tyranny!
Ambulance sirens?

The porn actress: Ambulance sirens with Dancing hookers! Because dAnCiNg-hOoKeRs-On-sTagE are Going to save the world with their vagina spaceships! So sometimes! So blueberries! Banana peels so Sexy with Unspeakable words! Eyeballs doing the Crazy dances with crazy Pizza! We must be prepared! Prepared with Orgasms! Prepared with Lots of facial expressions! Prepared with sUrReaLisT-pOrnOgRaPhiC-wOrDs jumping out of everything!

Otherwise, Gravity will be eaten by Little children! Otherwise, We will drink the blue sky until there is no blue sky! Otherwise, The darkness will haunt us with its beauty!

Give me my Testicles! And you! And you Must create art with a chainsaw & human bodies! And you all Can eat the planets &

suns & moons out of my ass! To some other planet you all!

I be building The greatest monument to schizophrenia ever! That's when I'm not Masturbating with all the 535 members of the United States Congress. Of course I'm Going to build a lunatic asylum on top of Mount Everest! I've never Had thousands of eyeballs in my head until today! But of course I have! I'm always Dancing seven days a week with all my readers!

The nun: I love your muShRooM-cLouD-hEad! Your muShRooM-cLouD-hEad is so charming! Do you Bathe neck deep in the tub with cum juices & pussy juices?

The porn actress: Do I? Of course! Which is, that the mass murderers jumping out of my penis, which is connected to the Zen Buddhism of circus clown farts, as far as Noisy-fornicating-cats at 4 AM goes, and when you add The Pornographic art of ancient Extraterrestrial civilizations, and you subtract Bullet holes in the walls, and you throw in a bunch of liViNg-dEad-pEopLe, but you leave out the everything fornicating under the Sun & Moon, and then you scream a bunch of red, and then you whisper a bunch of Diseased solar systems into your mother's ear while you're fucking her, well...

The nun: I see! But Siamese twins talking Philosophy with each other while masturbating! And you have an answer to New York City subway trains ending up at the Apocalypse?

The porn actress: Of course I have an answer to all that Bubblegum! The answer to New York City subway trains ending up in the Apocalypse, is more New York City subway trains ending up at the Apocalypse!

But then there's the Massive international shortage of diarrhea to think about. And there's also the Delightful car crashes while getting a blow job to consider. And we must never forget All those basketball teams using the decapitated head of Louis XVI to play basketball!

The nun: And what about dinosaurs Landing on The moon? And what about Silly words Landing on the Page? And what about Your balls itching with philosophy?

The porn actress: That's all Yesterday with lots of herpes! It's all a celebration of herpes! Unless, Nuclear war happens! And if nuclear war happens, Then it's the end of Jumping on the table and fucking the Thanksgiving turkey up the ass while the family watches!

But that would also be the beginning of Time with the Garden of Eden & lots of cum stains! And the beginning of Time with lots of cum stains, would cause lots of Dead people! And nobody wants that! Except for everybody!

You see, everybody Loves dead people! Giving grand speeches at drive-by shootings! And that's very Blow job from a Saint! But with lots of Pornographic Penguins jumping out of the Statue of Liberty's vagina!

Well it's been a pleasure Dancing with the dead people in the cemetery with you. Please have a pleasant Nuclear Armageddon!

75

You too!

The Italian Renaissance Slipping on a Banana Peel

Bugs Bunny Interviews The Dalai Lama while they Masturbate Together

Bugs Bunny Masturbating: You getting knocked in the head with Too many verbs? You Flying off to a big penis? I have a feeling that you Like People to pee on you?

The Dalai Lama Masturbating: I feel That when somebody pees on you it's a Spinning-vortex-kind-of-Experience! You feel Like a rock star whenever Somebody pees on you! We all feel Like rock stars when we pee on each other! It's a lot of

Medieval Knights charging into a Beatles concert. It's a lot of Giant erotic Nipples to roll up a hill. Sometimes, Your mother comes to me naked. But other times, Your father comes to me naked. Especially with lots of verbs & nouns swimming through the Air. Even now, The Tooth fairies are stealing all of our Penises.

Bugs Bunny: I heard you Crashed into the moon yesterday. Then you had sex with your own sister while you recited the periodic table of elements. You have a lot of Human bodies hanging from your ceiling at home?

The Dalai Lama: It's Raining with Schizophrenic alarm clocks! Sometimes with lots of Hungry alligators! The alligators Be swimming around the Poetry... The Wild monsters Jumping out of this poetry And devouring us. Our skin turns into time dripping & dripping into eternity. Even the Sexy 100-year-old grandmothers in French lingerie Are killing us with their machine guns!

Bugs Bunny: We can smell the coLLaPsiNg-cOllApSinG-coLLaPsInG of civilization all around us! The torrents of Smells so gabba-dabba-pappa with extra spices from hell! You Invented thousands of smells when?

The Dalai Lama: I always Smelled like a Space Elephant on crack! So much Noses in outer space to Smell with! So much now To masturbate with! Ferris wheels of Thousands of sexual fantasies! Now, Grab God by his Dick! So the question marks be flying like Spermatozoa! The elephants trampling all over the Wet dreams of Attila the Hun. It's Absolutely

Flying cats! It's lots of sunsets with your Hairy testicles! Sometimes, When the space aliens attack us we hide in God's anus. But that won't stop the Music!

Bugs Bunny: What do you think will stop the Space alien anuses from taking over modern literature? And how do we Cook our own brains on the stove?

The Dalai Lama: I find so much Hypocrisy in all our anuses! Then the Big anus of Jesus concerns me! I feel threatened by all the anuses attacking the planet Earth! Time is grabbing us! And we are all sickly with Computer viruses taking over our bodies! We build a bunch of sErIaL-kiLLer-cIviLiZaTiOnS. We try Hijacking all the Sunshine. Even the Sunlight is Filled with computer viruses! Only the winds of the past can Save us!

Bugs Bunny: But the winds of The past are Too schizophrenic! So what do you make of the The mushroom cloud getting bigger & bigger outside the window?

The Dalai Lama: The Smelly feet of all the Presidents of the United States of America will save us – save us from The hungry-Boiling-vats of City streets boiling over with Lunacy! The hands of Masturbation will save us from Flying saucers! The faces of The gargoyles on the buildings will explain all the neW-aWoKe-wOrdS to us! We have so much Evil to go! There is so much Wonderful evil to Stick Our Dick Into! Even my AK-47 is Having a good day!

Bugs Bunny: Do you feel the Hungry poetry eating through your stomach?

The Dalai Lama: I feel the Insanity eating through the Air. I feel the Who of me Somersaulting around the world! I feel the World zipping by me! Who else can Stick the world in his head like me? What Spirits of all the planets can be calling Me? And why not spray-paint obscene words In bright colors all over the walls of the city?

Bugs Bunny: Why not Paint obscene words everywhere? But The Wizard of The Scrotum sees everything! And who Do you think you are with those Thousands of faces In your face? And what Flood of the thousand hallucinations are you holding back?

The Dalai Lama: That's for the AK-47 in my hands To know! That's for My AK-47 To understand! The vIoLeNcE-oF-mY-sMiLe will devour! The Sunshine will conquer! So much Wild nights & crazy days to tell! I can't Hallucinate in PG-13!

I pee all over the liberal & conservative censors!

Nobel Prize Dildos for Tail-Waving Doggy-Woggys

Your cat interviews Your dog

Your cat: What the Boogers are you Thinking? How the Hallucinations suddenly appear all over the walls of the city?

You take an octopus with a thousand penises, add a bunch of Rocket launchers, eliminating all the gatekeepers in the way of artistic expression, and what do you got? You got a bunch of Creativity flooding across the world! And what about the Obscenity constantly bubbling-out-of-us?

Your dog: Well, The apocalypses of creativity is always Exploding out of our pens & paintbrushes! And that's Why poets & painters are vampires! And We should Take battering rams to the gatekeepers! But you gotta Watch out for the falling Pianos! Mozart with an AK-47 is especially dangerous!

Your cat: Are the hordes of invading Mozart clones dangerous because of Caffeine? Or is it dangerous because of the Art installations made of urine & feces covering the walls of the subway stations?

Your dog: Well, I like to think of it as storing my Penis in a time capsule. Now, Penis is Like a very excited verb! And, Pussy is Wet like the black ocean that surrounds the planet Earth! But that's only if The sun is gushing its rays through your wet dreams. And then there's the sexy moonlight to consider. Especially with all the Horny rabbits of Hell hopping around! Now, if the Masturbating birds in the trees is Okay with you, then it's obvious that Ejaculating endless mathematical equations out of our penises is the answer! And certainly, dragon brains melting everywhere is a factor.

Your cat: Certainly dragon brains taste good with Jackson Pollock's cum? And aren't you forgetting about the floors always disappearing under our feet?

Your dog: Well then, you don't get your fried cat testicles!

Your cat: Why is that?

Your dog: Because of the Gargoyles devouring our children as the parents applaud.

Your cat: Because of the Gargoyles devouring our children? But what about all the LSD trips through A thousand crucifixions of Christ? And the shifting balance of The Earth is Causing Cornflakes!

Your dog: Art museums really are delicious With or without Jackson Pollock's cum! That's why Gesundheit! And I believe that So much Hemingway will jump out of Your momma's tits! If only the Timing of the Nuclear war is right. And everyone believes that Getting drunk is the answer to nuclear Armageddon. So, since everyone believes that Getting drunk is wonderful with nuclear Armageddon, then Purple &

green polka dots everywhere! So if you throw in a bunch of Polka music as well, then Santa Claus with his big black Dick will Save us! You know that! It's as easy as Becoming a ghost!

Your cat: How could it be as easy as Becoming a ghost, if the Gorilla device on the buttocks machine is Haywire? And now, there's lots of Pink & blue flamingos making love to Ancient civilizations, have you considered that?

Your dog: No, because of Delicious cats in my pussy. It's as simple as this – Paint giant colorful vaginas all over the walls of the city! And how about Piano sonatas that taste like a prostitute's cum-filled vagina? Everybody wants some Prostitute's cum-filled vagina to eat! That's why we need to Start the Machines of Mass Murder going at once!

Your cat: But the Gorilla-booty-machine is threatening World peace! And that could cause The universe to fall apart! So how do you answer that?

Your dog: To that I say, Eat your own Life!

Human Brains for Dinner

An interview with A psychopath you just met

The reader: You Have smelly feet, or you Just farted Lots-of-wonder Out of your mouth? Because I can't understand your Out-of-this-Century Logic!

The psychopath: You No understand Out-of-this-Century Logic? How come This sPaCe-aLieN-aLpHaBeT is so Smelly? Or is it the Mental asylum filled with the greatest painters in the world? Anyway, Your mother fucked all them space aliens really good 9 months before you were born! It's so Wild-pubic-hairs with lots of

Suicide! And that's why tangerines! And that's why wrong-way street! Can you see the Words growing all over the sky? Because I can see the Words growing all over the sky! And that's why we be so Crazy with tomorrow! Now, about the Dead person in the trunk of your car, it's really Cold outside! And about the dead woman in your bed, well it's really Space alien to see ya! And that's why The Russian Czar is tap dancing on your grave! Can you see the Russian Czar tap dancing on your grave?

The reader: No! But I can see the Moon pissing it's Dixieland jazz all over You! And what about the Magical words that you've been smoking all day long? Have you thought about the Buttocks of the French aristocrats that want to be spanked today?

The psychopath: That's a lot of Doo-doo in your head! Or maybe it's a lot of Storm clouds over Your memories. Sometimes you just have to Masturbate on a public bus while everyone watches! But really, The Nobel Prize committee can all go fuck my mother Nine months before I'm born, because My mother is 90 years old! And that's why Dr. Seuss dancing naked through the Italian Renaissance is very white-male-patriarchy with lots of Cock-a-doodle-doo. But now, My train of a thousand personalities is coming! No, I mean Alice-in-Wonderland with a big black Dick between her legs, or is it A plane crash, I'm Not absolutely sure. But I'm absolutely sure that My dog's diarrhea on the ceiling of my apartment is a blessing from God! I can see the Words of the Bible jizzying all over my dog's face! Can you see the Words of the Bible jizzying all over my dog's face?

The reader: Hot tamales! This Sheep's pussy tastes like whipped cream! I can see the heaven above full of sexy sheep! And I can see the whipped cream around your balls. And what are your feelings about that?

The psychopath: My feelings about that are Lots of Socrates & Caligula Clones fucking each other up the ass. But only on days when My thoughts are percolating & percolating inside the readers' heads, or Days when You lose your brains in the toilet, or Nights when Your naked wife is chasing after Santa Claus. It's all God's punishment for my Masturbation sessions in front of Gorillas at the zoo. It's all really Lots of Baroque-rococo Brains with Springtime! Or maybe it's really Stupendous with lots of Female orgasms. But sometimes you just have to Tickle a grizzly bear's feet, until he laughs and eats you! Especially if the Moon is whispering to you about Masturbation and more Masturbation and more Masturbation!

The reader: I see. But Masturbation goes great with Musical tornadoes! And what about Your mother getting pregnant from a Bunch of Hells Angels 9 months before you were born?

The psychopath: That's Too much bananas up a chimpanzee's ass for me! It's really Human faces going around & around the washing machine! It's so Frantic with penises chasing each other! We must really Torch all tradition with the flames of our words! So Hippie-dippy with lots of crazy back-&-forth verbs! Or

Let's go skinny-dipping with a thousand hungry sharks!

The reader: But you haven't Chopped off my penis yet! Answer my Wisdom!

The psychopath: It's all about the Urine-smelling-alleyways. And then there's the Off-off-Broadway in Shakespeare's balls. But I'm absolutely Caffeinated with lots of zip! And you seem to be totally Full of worms. So, together, we should Shoot each other in the head!

The reader: That's impossible! There's so much Drugs in the sunshine! How do you feel about that?

The psychopath: I feel a bunch of Poetry orgasms coming on! Cunt-pussy-Bellybutton is making me feel Very choo-choo-train! And Spies are everywhere! So we Single men have to Understand

the Needs of hOrNy-seXy-wiVes!
Otherwise, a thousand languages will be
like a sea drowning us! And then there's
The thunder in the testicles to consider.
Like when the Decapitated human heads
in the refrigerator eat all the Endangered
species. So let's Exchange sexual
genitalia with the space aliens!

The reader: You Exchange sexual
genitalia with the space aliens? And why
don't you Smear the diarrhea of your
poetry all over the bathroom walls as
well?

The psychopath: Because I'm as horny
as a bologna sandwich! And always pigs
& chickens & cows falling out of my
booty hole! And yesterday I Lost my butt
to a lizard!

The reader: Too much Wisdom to eat out
of all the vaginas! We need more

tomorrow! Why don't you Shoot us With your crazy more tomorrow?

The psychopath: Shoot you more tomorrow? It's all Bullocks! Bullocks with lots of Murder sauce! So much tomorrow with Yesterday crashing through! That's why Words-on-a-page Masturbate constantly! And I'm okay with Masturbating with all the primates in the zoo.

The reader: Well I'm high in the clouds. How could anybody be okay with Masturbating with monkeys? Are you out of your Outer space?

The psychopath: Of course I'm out of my outer space! Everybody is out of their outer space!

10,000 pOpEs iN iTaLy maStuRbaTiNg tOgEthEr

An ant Interviews an elephant

The ant: I Jack off constantly! You jack off constantly?

The elephant: Murder and Love at the same time. Jacking off constantly While driving an 18 wheeler down the highway at the same time as well. You Play with those duckies! I Torpedo my spermatozoa across the Atlantic Ocean and into The aristocratic twat in the Buckingham palace!

The ant: That's the Millions-of-songs playing in your ears at the same time! So you must yes with lots of Feeling! And I must explain with lots of Diarrhea! And the birds in the sky must say Yes with so much Wisdom falling out of their booty holes and landing in our brains!

The elephant: We are all the Musical notes in a symphony called the human race! So much mOnSoOniNg-FeVeRish-aLphAbeT Bleeding everywhere!

The ant: But your face is Constantly-swirling-around-me right now! Is right now Even for real?

The elephant: Right now is As real as an orgy of a thousand-copulating-dogs on your doorstep! My face is Becoming So many sunrises! Your face is Becoming So much murder! The reader's face is Becoming So much music! And now, The music Tiptoes-across-The-day!

The ant: And now, Let's swim across an insomnia of words? But Colonel Sanders will fuck all the chickens of the world up the butt right now! Explain Chicken-fucking-up-the-butt-music! Explain Human faces that float out of these pages!

The elephant: Why don't I explain worms & vermin in my soul, instead? I mean, what the Craziness is the Time Machine sending us off to now?! I explain and I explain, but still the Bullets Sing by us! And still, The Murder continues with so much Compassion & brotherly love!

So, it's really about the Wisdom of the herpes sores on our penises! And sometimes, pSychOpaThiC-liGhtNinG-thOuGhtS happens! And so much Baroque-rococo Clouds on the ceiling to ride off to Sexy Land! Then All the rats in the walls will sing us a Sexy song! And that's how we find ourselves In somebody else's daydreams!

The ant: Find ourselves in somebody else's daydreams? No, I disagree! I think that Pineapples in everybody's vaginas is So circus! And I also think that Delicious Human meat with poetry is Very super! So, you're wrong!

The elephant: Of course I'm wrong! Because Of all of the uncircumcised penises! But that also makes me right too! You have to factor in all the Capitalist orangutans in all the corporate board rooms. Especially with all the Robots jumping out of our sex organs. And then add a bunch of Rolling hills & forests charging at you...

That way, Capitalist politics tastes like sadomasochism! And then we can Paint our vomit all over the walls of art galleries!

The ant: But that's so much Outer space orgasm! And outer space Orgasm is constantly happening! This is The third rail! What's the Rotting brains doing now?

The elephant: Because Of the Freight trains crashing into the imagination of Salvador Dali! Everyone must Fuck Salvador Dali's wife now! It's just not Snowing enough chaos! Jump up into A giant orgy in the heavens! And then you'll find The poetry of God's cum.

The ant: But if we find That delicious cheeseburger made out of dog meat, then Too much Silliness will happen! Isn't that true?

The elephant: Everything is true, and everything is false, because Of the Celestial nature of anal warts! And even if Your mother's pussy happens, we can always Have a barbecue with our neighbors absolutely naked. Or, we can Catch a bus of sexually transmitted diseases all the way to the White House in Washington DC. That's our plan.

The ant: The plan? I thought the plan was to Throw all of our sexually-transmitted diseases in a pile, and Then have a party?

The elephant: The plan was always to Do exactly that, but Then The traffic lights kept singing opera to us. That's why So much Breakfast cereal is happening!

The ant: But if so much Breakfast cereal is happening, what can we do about it?

And how come Your Planet Is
Disappearing?

The elephant: The Words excited with
sex is not the question! The question is
Should we ejaculate Democratic politics
or Republican politics into the pussy of
the First Lady! And then there's always
Chopped-off puppy tails to consider. But
that's only when The moon is blasting
spermatozoa Straight at us! Like just the
other day, it was lots of Science fiction
characters having anal sex everywhere in
my apartment! And, the day before that,
lots of Happy diseases on everybody's
faces! So you never know.

The ant: But we have to know! We have
to know if Our faces are going to melt
into Mathematical equations! And we
have to know if The computers are going
to invade our brains! Tell us! Tell us now!

The elephant: What I'll tell you now is that These words you're reading were planted into my brains by a space alien. And that's all I have to say.

The ant: That's all you have to say? But what about the Clouds in the sky whispering to us about Lots of nowhere?

The elephant: Hail these words dripping & dripping from our sexual organs! And the Rampaging pornography everywhere will take care of the Puppies eating puppies. And that's how we'll solve Gravity.

The ant: No, Gravity will not be solved by People jumping from skyscraper windows! Only the People jumping from skyscraper windows will solve the Mystery of Hot Dogs. Isn't that true?

The elephant: That's true, but only if You lose your ears on the other side of the moon. You have to consider the lions & tigers that live in your stomach.

The ant: But that's only true if Hopping frogs are hopping out of all of the pornography!

The elephant: No. Remember the Psychopathic Priests of The Attic! And remember the Buildings walking away from you! So everything will be Ecstasy!

The ant: Everything will be Ecstasy? But the Onslaught of Naughty school children is coming! And furthermore, deliriums & more deliriums & more deliriums happened! What do you have to say to that?

The elephant: Deliriums & more deliriums & more deliriums happen because of the Constant Sex between weather systems. Now if we subtract The tropical rain forests of your crotch from Hot dog stands, and we multiply that by oVeRseXed-dOgs-eVerYwheRe, and then we throw in a bunch of iTchY-gEniTaL-cRabS, we'll get Drunken piss Smelling alleyways full of pagan gods!

The ant: Oh! I see! That makes perfect sense!

Ronald McDonald & Jesus Christ Meet in Boys Town

Ronald McDonald interviews Jesus Christ

Ronald McDonald: You jumping out of Spaceships every day? You flying out of Reality? What you think of Pussy Goddess Galore?

Jesus Christ: I be jumping out of Spaceships, because The dogs be Reading my brains! I be flying out of Reality, because of hallways & more hallways & more hallways going everywhere! That's my Universe!

Ronald McDonald: But The cats are meowing from outer space! And George

Washington & the founding Fathers in our balls want Big Mac & large fries & Coke! What Howling dogs now?

Jesus Christ: That's why dragonflies taste crunchy! And Flying words around Is so up & up & up! That's the Way to civilizations that don't exist yet!

Ronald McDonald: But sometimes the calligraphy we Spurt all over the walls is So delightfully pornographic! Why the Eyeballs in your face? Why Those feet of yours on the ground? And why the ears in your head going East & West?

Jesus Christ: Sometimes my mother is too sexy for me to resist her! Other times 10,000 erections are parading down the street! And at all times, Tipsy-Turvy Holidays are So cocaine! That's the Smelly feet of it! That's the Train speeding to somebody else's schizophrenia! And that's why Capitalism tastes like barbecued doo-doo!

Round McDonald: That's a lot of Honey in the butt! It's also a lot of sailing into Naughty seas! So, how much For a blow job?

Jesus Christ: How much a Blow job? That's the Priest on fire screaming down the street! It's also the Fishing for ice cream In a space monster's vagina! And now the Sweet executions everywhere! So, I just like to say, Your farts smell like French Impressionism! And lots of 1970s!

Ronald McDonald: Lots of 1970s? And what about lots of Used condoms? And did you forget the Space alien abductions?

Jesus Christ: I didn't forget the space alien abductions! And I also didn't forget the Sex with strangers in alleyways for mOneY-MoNeY-mOneY! Who could forget the Trees of Schizophrenia growing out of Everybody's imagination? Can anybody forget the clouds in the sky On fire?

And that's why I say it's time for Playing with switchblade knives! It's time for Romantic knife slashings under the moonlight! And it's time for Preaching the Glory of sex & more sex & more sex! Smells! Slash! Barbecue!

Ronald McDonald: Smells? Slash? Barbecue? Are you Hi on Gothic architecture? Or are you A motherfootor with a studio apartment filled with human skulls?

Jesus Christ: I'm a Space alien from the garbage can! And I'm also a Fish from your mother's vagina! And I'll always be Having intergalactic sex with your wife! So, think of me as a Big genital wart Growing out of the Central intelligence agency!

Ronald McDonald: You are, of course, a Big genital wart walking around on two legs! I think of you as a Perfectly sane person with lots of Boogie-woogie-Oggie-Oggie! Pornography? And more Pornography? Fresh paint?

Jesus Christ: I like to Do pornography with My religion! I yes Have pornography with all The Jesus Christ! Whip me! Whip me! The electric chair With lots of Cherry pie! So everybody Continue the conversations in their own heads right now!

Ronald McDonald: Everybody Continue the conversations in their own heads right now?

Jesus Christ: Yes.

How to Seduce a Skunk

God interviews a Goat

God: It's a jazz Dizziness, no? Or yes? Is it a bunch of lions & tigers devouring each other?

The goat: A bunch of Lions & tigers devouring each other? Look, baby, how cRazY-taLkiNg-coLLage is that?! Too many pajamas! Lots of bananas! It's so Afternoon delicious with bloodshed!

God: Yes, but...

The goat: But Too many grasshoppers everywhere! You see All the vaginas attacking outer space? You see the Screams that nobody can hear? You hear the paintings? You smell the words dripping off the pages? Everybody singing rock 'n' roll from the electric chair! Everybody dAnCiNg-dOwN-tHe-sTreEt while they're swinging those machetes! That's why Sports is so fun! It's no good without the Flying electric chairs everywhere!

God: But sometimes Even my masturbations create symphonies! Symphonies so Cherry & sweet! How come The cemetery is full of Gothic literature percolating everywhere?

The goat: Like the rhythms of Funky-white-boys doing black, everything is Up the sky! Like the sights of Baroque-rococo whorehouses, It's all Very Martian! So much Very Martian for everyone! So much Very Martian for no one! Russian roulette is the answer!

God: Russian roulette is the answer?
Then what's the question?

The goat: Well, that's why you're here!
To ask questions! Ask me questions
about anal sex! Ask me questions about
Ice-skating in heaven! And what about
the Forever suns in the sky that keep
Loving us? Why not ask me about that?
Or ask me about the Mushroom clouds
coming tomorrow!

God: I'd like to ask you about the
Mushroom clouds coming tomorrow!

The goat: So ask me! And while you ask
me I'll dance! I'll dance to the yEast
infections in everybody's vaginas! I'll
dance to Hiroshima & Nagasaki! And
then I'll Chop off my own head! And then
we can all Have a vacation inside of a
madhouse known as the White House!

God: The nuthouse/White House is so
Flowers growing out of nuclear missiles!
But then again, everything is so Flowers
growing out of nuclear missiles! Don't
you think so?

The goat: I think! And I think! And I
think! I think that Jumping from rooftop
to rooftop at three in the morning is
Divine! And I think that Corpses look so
attractive in French lingerie! But I never
ever ever Kiss a Black hole in outer
space!

God: You never ever ever Fuck a duck?
But without the Fook a duck, how do you
Obtain outer space?

The goat: How do I Obtain outer space?
Well I Snort my mother up my nose, and
I Snort all of French Impressionism up
my nose, and then I Snort all the Noise-
in-the-world up my nose! Circles and

circles of Cocaine flying everywhere!
Mathematical Murder up high! Delirious
deliriums down low! And naKed-
hAndSomE-meN everywhere!

God: And naKed-hAndSomE-meN
everywhere? But what about the Angry
Characters jumping out of novels and
marauding down the streets everywhere?

The goat: Well the Angry Sunshine that's
everywhere, is not the same as the
naKed-hAndSomE-meN that's
everywhere! Even a fish knows that!

God: But do the fish know How to cook
up a batch of meth? And do the monkeys
know All the thousands of doorways into
each other's minds? And do the Ducks in
the pond know That they are inside your
brains?

The goat: Who knows? But, lots of
Herpes for everyone! Lots of Herpes with
your Baloney sandwich, you know?
Everybody knows! Everybody knows that
The big herpes Apocalypse In the sky will
save us from Thinking! And nobody
knows that Herpes sores make great
philosophers! And the fish & monkeys &
elephants all know that Nuclear
apocalypse tastes like 100-year-old
pussy! Do you know that Your insides will
soon be dribbling all over the sky?

God: Aren't I supposed to ask the
questions?

The goat: You should play soccer with
my decapitated head! Then you should
Chop off my penis and use it to fuck your
wife! And after that, you should Jump
into a toilet bowl and never come back!
And then –

God: No I shouldn't! But what I should do is Have a big party with my murderers before they murder me! And you should Too! What do you say to that?

The goat: I say that Dancing on top of the moon as it rolls down the alleyway is So summertime! And I say that Monkey brains taste great with a summer breeze! And I can hear the fish in the ocean saying that this Genocide is sweet! And I can hear the monkeys in the zoo Calling each other four letter names! And I can even hear the clouds in the sky saying Goodbye to the human race!

God: WOW! Your hearing is really Zoo crazy with Morning showers! Can you hear the Wisdom Of the meth addicts?

The goat: Of course! Everybody can hear that! And I can even hear the Farts of

Leonardo da-vinci from hundreds of years ago! And I can smell My own death! And I can also smell the silent Angry tirades of Everyone! But sometimes the smells of Angry tirades become so Contagious! And Contagious is Everywhere! So Firing squad!

God: I see, well let's both jump into a volcano now!

The goat: Great! Let's do it!

*The Reader & the Writer Sniff Glue
Together*

An interview

The reader: Man, Why you so Lost-in-the-forest with me? And why Do the birds all have the faces of Charles Manson?

The writer: I'm telling you man, the Weather is On fire, and that's why I Eat Your dreams, especially with all Telephone calls from God, and then there's all that Egyptian hieroglyphics in my food, and that's why I have Supernatural powers, and now There's

122

porcupines crawling all over my skin, you see?

The reader: Man, you Shouldn't be playing so much Russian Roulette with yourself! So why don't you Pounce on me?

The writer: No, why don't you Pounce on me instead?! You know what the problem is with people like you? You don't Have midnight orgies with barn animals! You always Jump from psychedelic revolution to psychedelic revolution! You don't understand that The frogs in your brains are always talking to me! But me, I'm always a Marie Antoinette drag queen in Times Square New York City during the 1970s! You got it?

The reader: Yeah, I got it! But then you Used to be John Wayne Gacy! How you going to explain that?

The writer: What I'm explaining is that, All the Pope's pooh-poohs are all Glorious! Always Open the Doorways of your imagination! Anyway, I be Playing thE-eNd-Of-tHe-wOrLd-mUsiC with 10,000 singing cats at 3 in the morning. And 10,000 singing cats be joined in this music by foaming-at-the-mouth rabid barking dogs! Can't you see the Volcanoes of sex Spewing all over the earth? Everybody can see the Winds of evil tapping us on the shoulder!

The reader: Bird droppings, I See the Tasty music! But what you sayin' is So patriotic with Wet pussy! And the problem with that is, it's all this Panic rumbling through the Women's panties! You see what I'm saying?

The writer: Yeah, I see what you sayin'! But what about All the Diseases we

want? You gotta consider *that* Paradise
of sexual bubonic plagues! And always
My skin be itching with politics! And
sometimes A strange thought will eat me
alive! And eArThQuaKeS-oF-thOughTs go
round and round My head! That way, you
don't Discover the diarrhea-filled toilet
bowl that will lead you to The Truth!
Especially with all this Singing from the
Choir of Crack Addicts!

The reader: I see your point. But now,
people are worried about Birds eating
them. And other people are worried
about Being suddenly swallowed by the
Sky. What do you say to them?

The writer: I say that Sexually
transmitted diseases are wonderful with
blueberry pie! And I also say that
Slipping on a banana peel all the way to
the whorehouse is Fabulous! Because

tomorrow! Tomorrow so much bOuNciNg-oRaNgUtaN-bOOty is going to happen! All that bOuNciNg-oRaNgUtaN-bOOty is going to happen with so much Lovely diseases! Lovely diseases for all to share! That's why I Love to see Car crashes! Especially with the children Devouring their teachers with ravenous hunger! The children are going to go On a murdering spree! And the adults are going to go Circus-crazy-with-cuckoo-clocks! We gotta Jump the space shuttle to somewhere else in the universe right away!

The reader: But how are we going to Eat lots of pussy, when God has eaten all the pussy, and there is no more pussy left to eat?

The writer: Falling bombs from heaven is So beautiful day? Say what? That's Lots of cuckoo! That's crazy with a lot of Kingdom Cum! That's so crazy that I'll kiss your smelly feet! I mean, what's wrong with you?! Are you saying that We should be normal? Because that's totally wrong! We need to right all the wrongs with Lots of nipples!

The reader: How are we going to Right all the wrongs with a bunch of Diarrhea? We need More rabid dogs biting us in the ass, and we need it yesterday! You disagree?

The writer: It's not a question of Dog-eating-contests (the 4-legged kind), it's a question of Sticking your Dick into all the holes in the walls! We need more Holes in the walls for all our Dicks! And we need Fluorescent prostitute Vaginas with whipped cream! Right?! So, first we Chop off all our body parts, then we Sell our body parts to The Pope, and then after that we can Go on holiday, and that'll cause Lots of bonkers to happen, which in turn will encourage lots of Jumping off of Cliffs, and with lots of Jumping off of Cliffs, then we'll achieve Instant gratification!

The reader: That sounds nice in theory. But what about the Screaming monsters in Your attic?

The writer: I'm not worried about the Screaming monsters in My attic! You see, with all this cHaOs-iN-ouR-hEads, and all that Dog pooh of liberalism & conservativism, and with so much Hallucinations going around, I think we need to worry about Being eaten by our own mouths.

The reader: I see. Well thank you for appearing on our Pornographic show today.

The writer: It's been my pleasure to Engage in pornography With you.

The Rollercoaster of Penis & Pussy

My Buttocks Interview The Virgin Mary

My Buttocks: It's the whole everything With lots of Deadly Spices! You feel Like Flying off to a whole new Fantasy of sexual depravity Today?

The Virgin Mary: Yes! Yes! Yes! All the yes is Sexually gratifying with fried chicken! So much everything to lick & lick & lick at all hours of the day & night! All the everything is descending on us! Us! Us! Us! We are all painters of thoughts! It's so much yes, that I want to Jump into a thousand volcanoes today! It's so much everything, that we all want to Become some other species living halfway across the universe!

My Buttocks: You seem rather Shoot-somebody-in-the-head Today! Is that because the sunshine makes you Become other people on other planets?

The Virgin Mary: Yes to the Virgin Mary making pornography with a black man while My husband God watches! And yes to so much Gonorrhea! So much Television commercials in my butt to See! We've got to have a lot of everything! We have to have a whole lot of everything Going wild everywhere! And that way, we will unite all the Spermatozoa of all the men on the planet! And we'll unite all the Rats of the world Together! We'll create sex with poetry! All the Sexually transmitted diseases will be united as one!

My Buttocks: Are you referring to the big brain of Humanity floating in outer space?

The Virgin Mary: The big brain of Humanity is upon us! With the combined big brain of humanity we'll All be a giant noun! It will be so much mUsiCaL-bOdY-oRgAnS! We will unite the universe into a Big toilet! We will unite everybody's thoughts into a Big toilet! Think of it! All the human thought united into a big Heap of manure! Think of all the Maggots crawling in our brains! It's a whole lot of Poetry & maggots!

My Buttocks: A whole lot of Poetry & maggots? But, The 12 tone scale of Arnold Schonberg is delicious with dirty-smelly-panties! And your critics say that Your dirty-smelly-panties taste like Chocolate when they lick them!

The Virgin Mary: To My Balzac with all my critics! They can all Be ejaculated into the mouth of some stranger in the park at night! With feet we borrow from other people, we all climb Through a bizarre plot that's flooding out of this novel. With Onslaughts of music we fly into each other's brains! With Doo-doo we build giant sculptures of a thousand years of wisdom! A thousand years of wisdom That smells like fresh doo-doo on a hot summer day!

My Buttocks: But with a thousand years of wisdom come Raindrops of cum. And how do you respond to the Lizards Who claim that You stole the dinosaur age?

The Virgin Mary: I respond with My Dick peeing American manifest destiny All over them! And I respond with Lots of shouts of glee! All the everything that

I'm carving into these walls is so much Emotion! A Monstrous-circling-world-of-thought is upon us every second! A Catastrophe of Cock-a-doodle-doo is upon us every hour! The Giant Aurora borealis Of sex is upon us every day! We must do something! We must do something with all the Penises!

My Buttocks: But Penises Are so Up-and-down with this music! So, why drive-by shootings on this beautiful sunny afternoon?

The Virgin Mary: Because Of Penis cannibalism! So much unity to Penis with! It's all the everything of the world in one little Noun! And one little Noun is a big Penis! A big Penis to charge into the Dark dungeon Of bourgeois morality!

My Buttocks: Charge into the Dark dungeon of bourgeois morality? Are you crazy with Lots of penis?

The Virgin Mary: Of course I'm crazy with Lots of penis! And I'm also crazy with Pussy! I'm a good crazy! I'm the good crazy of The world! We need more good crazy! We need more good crazy Chaos! Good crazy Chaos for all!

My Buttocks: Good crazy Chaos for all? But then, everybody will Kill everybody, no?

The Virgin Mary: Yes! And that's a good thing! Everybody killing everybody is a good thing! All the Killing is a good thing! Lots of good things Come from Killing people! And the good things will topple each other! And we will build good things so high that Banana peels! Whirlpooling-good-things Going ha-ha-ha! So much good things that Everyone leaps into Hieronymus Bosch paintings!

My Buttocks: But, let me ask you, what about the Year of the Delicious Cat?

The Virgin Mary: That's Science fiction with lots of pornography! Or, it's Pornography with lots of poetry! Either way, so much Pornography to put smiles on the animals' faces! And now – As my next trick – I'm going to make the planet Earth disappear!

My Buttocks: Well, the nuclear bombs will be arriving any moment now. It's been fun!

The Virgin Mary: It's been fun with Trains crashing into each other! It's been fun with Lots of humans to eat! And so much fun with Paintbrushes creating brightly-colored Shakespearean dialogue dancing

everywhere! It was nice to live while we
could!

Shakespeare Drinking Cheap Vodka with A Self-Proclaimed Jesus Christ that isn't Jesus Christ

Drunken Shakespeare: What wild Jesus Christ faces everywhere? When the Crucifixion party? Who is You?

Jesus Christ that isn't Jesus Christ: Too much You! It's not Up-or-down to be seasick in This alleyway! You know who is the Conqueror of the invisible universe?! It's the Bedbugs! And that's why I be Homeless! You dig? Because you got to dig and dig Until all that Boogers come out of you! And now I'm going to be captain of this vodka bottle straight into outer space!

Drunken Shakespeare: Yeah, but Vomit is full of wisdom! And what you say to that Girl over there with so many fluorescent vaginas floating out from under her miniskirt?

Jesus Christ that isn't Jesus Christ: I say that 2+2 equals the end of the world! And everybody else can just Kiss the ass of Jesus Christ! Because of the seagulls – those birds are such smart asses! Sometimes, I find myself having a party with all the Nuns in the whorehouse, and we're all drinking vodka together! So We do a lot of aBsTraCt-eXpResSiOniSt-seX to each other! No more Daylight when you can just wipe your ass with Lots of verbs! Yes to Bedbugs and snot all over your capitalist politics!

Drunken Shakespeare: But then, We'd find ourselves drinking this vodka on the moon together! Is that why That rat scurrying over there is The ghost of George Washington?

Jesus Christ that isn't Jesus Christ: Why the ghost of George Washington? And why the Siamese twins hanging by the ceiling in your garage? And why the Garbage smell like Installation art? And why the Urine smell like Minimalism?

Drunken Shakespeare: Exactly! Why?

Jesus Christ that isn't Jesus Christ: Because of the Herpes on my penis!

Drunken Shakespeare: But that doesn't make any Egyptian hieroglyphics! Don't you think that God's mind is delicious?

Jesus Christ that isn't Jesus Christ: Who would think that!? Everybody is Higher than the clouds in Your brain! And nobody is Stealing each other's testicles yet! All the streets Be Allergic to me! With so many oceans of Spermatozoa swimming around us! And so many asteroids of Cunnilingus! You gotta march to the beating drums of the cunnilingus monsters! Or you gotta pee on yourself!

Drunken Shakespeare: Then Everything will swallow you up! Who Is conducting this Symphony of Civil War?

Jesus Christ that isn't Jesus Christ: That's a Salami & cheese kind of question! There's all kinds of questions. There is Dagger-in-your-brains kind of questions. And then there's Hang-yourself-from-a-tree kind of questions.

Drunken Shakespeare: Right. So answer the question!

Jesus Christ that isn't Jesus Christ: I'll answer the question, if All the mermaids in the sea give me a blow job! And then, only if They swallow! Let's cook each other's dead bodies over a campfire!! Be really Honest with your pubic hairs! And then, Your salvation is lots of Buttocks running around! Then Drinking happens! So it's all very Buttocks.

Drunken Shakespeare: Drinking is very Glorious buttocks! So that's a lot of Blow jobs from all the politicians of your country! You Lost in the maze of my words?

Jesus Christ that isn't Jesus Christ: Me? I be finding Your clones Everywhere! And tomorrow, I be all Zigzagged with Choo-choo trains! There's no way that tomorrow is going to even happen! There ain't going to be no tomorrow!

Drunken Shakespeare: But if there ain't going to be no tomorrow, then why not Tattoo oBsCeNe-wOrdS-aLL-oVeR-yOuR-sKin Now?! So what do you think of that?

Jesus Christ that isn't Jesus Christ: I ain't thinking at all! It's all about the instincts in my balls! And the instincts in my balls be telling me Lots of Paradises!

Drunken Shakespeare: Is that What the instincts in your balls be telling you? Then what do the instincts in your balls tell you about Schizophrenic robots?

Jesus Christ that isn't Jesus Christ: Let me ask my balls. Hey balls: 'what you think about Schizophrenic robots?' Okay! I'm listening to my balls! And my balls are telling me that Sistine-Chapel-homoerotic-orgies is Great! And my balls are also saying that Painting homoerotic art all over the walls of all the cities of the world is the answer!

Drunken Shakespeare: Well, your balls are very wise! Let me ask you both a question. Hey balls of this dude sitting across from me, what the Crazy cuckoo clock be the Answer?

The man's balls say: Well, it's all about Leonardo Da Vinci's spermatozoa. Really, lots of Spermatozoa with your Kindness! Too much Spermatozoa with your Poetry! Not enough Spermatozoa with your Lunch & dinner! Polish sausage! Floating Daydreams! Forever Nightmares!

Drunken Shakespeare: Well, let me ask you balls another question, if I may?

Jesus Christ that isn't Jesus Christ: Go ahead.

Drunken Shakespeare: What is the answer to Being everywhere at the same time?

The balls of Jesus Christ that isn't Jesus Christ: The Answer is Eat out the Mona Lisa's vagina in the Louvre.

Drunken Shakespeare: Well, there you have it! This dude's balls say that Eating out the Mona Lisa's vagina in the Louvre is the answer to everything! And this concludes today's edition of "Burn Down the Literary Establishment".

A Mouse Interviews a Cat

The mouse: You eat Words dribbling &
squiggling everywhere? What you do
about Nuclear missiles dribbling &
squiggling everywhere?

The cat: I kill! I Dance with the Festering
Bonfires Of War! I kill the Sunny
sunshine of Your dreams! Always!
Yesterday! Too much!

The mouse: I see. But Pineapples!
Deranged! Tomorrow! A bloody knife in
your hand?

The cat: A bloodied knife in my hand is
so Smiling Priest! Scrambled-brains-of-a-
world! Yes! So much maybe! Helicopter

up Your wet dreams! Lake of Glistening blood! That's a sweet death!

The mouse: You having a wet dream right now?

The cat: No! Lots of no with Lots of wet dreams! And maybe! Lots of maybe with a Guitar playing Your violent death! So much night sky to Shoot my Pleasure all over. So much morning to Devour! Where the Hungry is. And now!

The mouse: And now Screaming screams so Turbulent?

The cat: Lots of maybe! There's Screams all about! That's why car crashes!! Car crashes and more car crashes and more car crashes!!! The car crashes help us to Think. But then the sun rises and Drools psychopathic thoughts All over the earth. And then the moon Commits suicide.

The mouse: So what to do?

The cat: Well, there's always Fire trucks. Sometimes, You're falling into some kind of everywhere! Watch out! Watch out for the Emptiness! Empty afternoons! The Empty afternoons be Stampeding everywhere! So you must be aware! Be aware of Your life galloping away from you! And be aware of the Time Machine devouring you!

The mouse: Time Machine devouring us? Really!

The cat: It's true! It's true with so much Death a little more each day! Also true with Thoughts evaporating out of our heads! That's why we devour! We devour and we devour and we devour! If we no devour, then Monsters happens! And if Monsters happens, then So much joy for the Torpedoes of love! Now, if you add a bunch of Empty hallways filled with ghosts, and kill a bunch of Sunny afternoons, and then suicide! Suicide and more suicide and more suicide! Now!

The mouse: But now is lots of Schizophrenic normality! No?

The cat: Lots of questions! Answers! Answers of Musical notes floating around this afternoon! Answers of Bullets shooting through the musical notes! But then there is this tornado! And there's all this margarine! What to Ride across the Seas of blood with, I don't know! I don't know if This sunshine is poisoning me with reality! Only the Cockroach crawling down my leg knows! And the Other cockroach crawling Up my leg knows if I'm delicious or not. Eat yourself! Eat yourself with lots of Cockroaches!

The mouse: Lots of Cockroaches? But what about the cities & planets & Wet dreams headed towards us at full speed?

The cat: Nobody can Predict Which planet we'll be on tomorrow! So we must stab all the nobody! Stab and stab and stab! Knives of Knowledge! Knives of Paradise! And knives of Slash & Stab & death! When you're carving somebody up with your knife it's like Being king of the moment! Death! Let us worship death! Death is the Sweet song summoning us!

The mouse: But if there's Too many naughty nouns in the literary batter, then bananas & more bananas & more bananas will happen! Yes?

The cat: So much yes with Bananas! So much Bananas with Everything flying

everywhere around us! So much
Everywhere with lots and lots of Now!
That's why Winter & Summer are making
love! And Winter & Summer making love
is so much War! So much Love with
Cannonballs! We have to go up & up &
up!

The mouse: But lots of up & up & up is
down! Too much up is down! So, What's
the Air-raid-Sirens, airrRRrrr-raiddDDdd-
SireeeeEEEeeens, aaaAAaaair-rrRRrraid-
SirennnNNNNnnns?

The cat: That's Everything disappearing
at once! The answer is to stab and stab
and stab! Gunshots! Murder! Murder with
Smiles everywhere! Murder with
Laughter everywhere! It's okay to be
psycho if you're Funny with your killing!
If you're Funny with your killing, then

everything will be okay with lots of Blood!

The mouse: But if everything's okay, then everything will go wrong! Isn't that true with lots of Things that go psycho?

The cat: I eat lots of Things that go psycho! That's why I can Juggle half-A-dozen Homicidal tendencies at the same time! Nobody else can Do that while they're whistling the tune "Psychopathic Love With Whips & Handcuffs"! That's what makes me as special as Any serial killer! Open Sesame!

The mouse: Blood? Sweet-smiling-knife-blade? Too much Death carrying you away?

The cat: Psycho is delicious with Bathing in a hot tub full of human blood! If you don't understand that, then Up the planet Mars with you! You have to see The future with your zippy eyes! Your zippy eyes will make The Future happen! With so much Future happening, all the Future will fester everywhere. Death is everyone! There's so much everyone that Eating Daily human flesh Is possible! There's so much everything that I love you! When you have so much everyone, then Zombies can happen! That's So Murder & murder & murder that Everything is collapsing! Give me your bellybutton please!

The mouse: I no kiss This Reality! You In outer space on this?

The cat: That depends on which day of the week it is. Because on Mondays, there's lots of Pornography to eat! But on Tuesdays, there's never enough Space alien prostitutes jumping out of flying saucers! Lots of Wednesdays! Too many Wednesdays! We need less Wednesdays! And sometimes Thursday never happens! And when Thursdays never happens, then Ski-across-heaven for everyone! And then there's all that Wednesday stuff happening on Saturdays. Fridays are sometimes devoured by American presidential candidates from Satan's dungeon. What can you do?

The mouse: You can Name all the zombies in the United States Congress! Can you?

The cat: Yes! You can Go ice-skating through Hell with all those zombies. All you need is lots of Thursdays! But it's kind of hard to find Thursdays, especially with all this Inflation!

The mouse: Well thank you for the Inflation!

The cat: You're welcome with lots of Outhouses!

Your Mother Interviewing Your Father As They Conceive You in the Backseat of a Car

Your Mother: So what you think of Driving a car off a cliff on purpose?

Your Father: I think that These computers need to stop growing out of our heads! But my butt disagrees! My butt thinks that Computer viruses taste good. But my testicles disagree with my butt! My testicles think that You're cute. But my smelly feet disagree with my testicles! My smelly testicles think that Des Moines Iowa is heaven on earth!

156

Your Mother: So who do you think is right? You, your butt, your testicles, or your smelly feet?

Your Father: Well, right now God is communicating to me via The windshield wipers of my car.

Your Mother: And what is God saying?

Your Father: God is saying that Pablo Picasso is up there in heaven sucking the big black Dick of the Virgin Mary. But my farts disagree with God.

Your Mother: Oh yeah? Why is that?

Your Father: My farts are saying Grace. But right now Satan's spermatozoa are communicating to me via the afterlife.

Your Mother: And what is Satan's spermatozoa saying?

Your Father: Satan's spermatozoa is saying that Having a family is like having a grenade lodged up your butt. But Roman Emperor Nero just chopped off Mick Jagger's head at this moment. And Nero is saying that Relatives taste a lot like Sewer rats. But a squirrel in the park just ate Nero, and Richard Nixon is saying that The Roman Emperor Nero tastes a lot like Romantic era symphonies.

Your Mother: That's cool that you have telepathy like that. How do you get telepathy?

Your Father: You get telepathy by Sucking lots of cock. And then people in the afterlife communicate with you via this fuck machine. This fuck machine is operated by thousands of monkeys. All the monkeys have Computers as heads.

You see, space aliens Born from your herpes sores become capitalist politicians. And the Faces of the Politicians replace the original Faces of the monkeys.

Your Mother: And why did the space aliens do that?

Your Father: Because the space aliens have herpes.

Your Mother: But how did the space aliens get herpes?

Your Father: The space aliens got herpes from the 535 members of Congress. You see the 535 members of Congress were traveling to a fairytale. But then they were eaten by a lizard that's suffering from schizophrenia.

Your Mother: Where did the lizard's schizophrenia come from?

Your Father: It came from My vacations in the public toilet.

Your Mother: I see, so the Exploding nouns on the walls of the public toilet were infected with schizophrenia?

Your Father: Yes, because Of John F. Kennedy! You see, the gonorrhea of Jesus Christ, and the syphilis of John F. Kennedy, combined together when Hitler invaded Poland. This happened in a homosexual bathhouse.

Your Mother: What was The homosexual bathhouse called?

Your Father: It was called "The Seas of Cum". At the Seas of Cum so-called "happenings" were performed. At the happenings, there was Lots of monkeys & porn stars & priests from the Church of Satan. There was fellatio performed by transsexual pumpkins with 12 legs each. And there was an opera written by a homeless man living in the park and conducted by a very horny porn actress.

Your Mother: Who performed the happenings?

Your Father: A bunch of Teenagers with AK-47s. Also a bunch of Catholic priests that were naked under their robes. And also a bunch of Murdering poets with big axes in their hands.

Your Mother: Sounds very Normal for an ex-dockworker like you. Did any Queen of England clones with big black Dix participate as well?

Your Father: Yes. All the members of the English royal family participated as Porn actors. And then there was the Green & purple colored midget With a very well-endowed Cock-a-doodle-doo. They All did a pornographic musical together on Broadway.

Your Mother: And how did the Virgin Mary feel about this?

Your Father: The Virgin Mary was Screaming out crazy shit at the top of her lungs the whole time. She was there as the Queen of Yeast Infections. And then there was the pagans.

Your Mother: What did the pagans do?

Your Father: The pagans did a lot of Masturbation with exotic objects loaned to them from the space aliens. The Pagans also did a lot of Flag burning, particularly the American flag. The Virgin Mary joined them, and together they did a lot of Cocaine.

162

Your Mother: How did Satan figure in all of this?

Your Father: Satan was there with God. Together, Satan and God were Snorting lots of cocaine. They were also Doing a very naughty double penetration of my mother, Who's 90 years old. And sometimes All three of them would perform a pornographic version of the State-of-the-Union address together. Other times, Satan would hang out with the President of the United States of America.

Your Mother: What was the President of the United States of America like?

Your Father: He was very Sexy. When the President of the USA & Satan would have anal sex together, the Virgin Mary would sing the Opera of Anal Sex. Jesus Christ would be on drums playing Lots-of-craziness. And all of the 535 Congresspeople would be Performing all kinds of bizarre-sexual-rituals with the corporate lobbyists.

Your Mother: That sounds very Normal for a planet like ours! Anything else happen?

Your Father: Yes there would be ritualistic human sacrifices. It was lots of fun! When the ritualistic human sacrifices were being performed, Jesus Christ & the American President would ejaculate all over the People being sacrificed, after first getting a blow job from the Virgin Mary.

Your Mother: Did the Virgin Mary ever blow you?

Your Father: Oh yes! Lots of times!

Your Mother: Did the Virgin Mary give good head?

Your Father: Oh, the Virgin Mary gave fantastic head! Her blow jobs were like One of Hunter Biden's paintings!

Your Mother: Did the Virgin Mary swallow?

Your Father: Hell yeah! You know Who also Gives fantastic Head is the American President! When the American president is giving you head you feel like 10,000 laughing monkeys! You feel like You're the first human to ever live! Hey, I'm getting rather excited! Do you mind if I Shoot my load into you? I know you're not on birth control, but who cares! I mean, you're married and all. It'll turn out all right!

Your Mother: Sure! Go ahead! Cum in me!

Your Father: Okay! Here we go!

What Does Cat Taste Like?

A Vibrator interviews 10,000 clones of
Adam & Eve

The Vibrator: So what you do?

The 10,000 clones of Adam & Eve all
respond together: I Spit! I Play piano
with my penis every afternoon! And then
I Ejaculate my poetry all over the faces
of the passerby on the street! I do lots of
Verbs! But I don't do enough Drive-by
shootings! You got Some chlamydia for
me?

The Vibrator: Yeah, I got some sexually
transmitted diseases. You want some?

The 10,000 clones respond together: I love sexually-transmitted diseases! I love sexually-transmitted diseases so much that I have my own sexually-transmitted diseases opera house! You can Sing lots of liberal & conservative politics with sexually-transmitted diseases!

The Vibrator: Speaking of sexually-transmitted diseases, what you think of capitalist politicians?

The 10,000 clones: Capitalist politicians are the wrong kind of sexually transmitted diseases! Because with sex you have fun! Ain't nothing fun about capitalist politicians! All the Capitalist politicians can kiss my Herpes!

The Vibrator: Speaking of kissing Herpes, what you think of Capitalism?

The 10,000 clones: I think it be like Aiming a Giant-penis-monster at the mirror and pulling the trigger. But only if God blesses you with a bunch of Herpes First. So, I got a lot of Glow-in-the-dark sex objects from The space aliens. I mix it up with the Pepper & salt. And that's how I get High! Presto! Bing-bong! That's some Sexy peanut butter for you all!

The Vibrator: Some Sexy peanut butter for us all? How you gonna Travel into my imagination with that?

The 10,000 clones: I'm a gonna Blow up the moon with that! And then I'm going to Take the pieces of the moon and build lots of oVeRseXeD-zOmBie-aRchiTeCtuRe! Especially on Syphilis Tuesdays! Because Syphilis Tuesdays is when everybody Discovers thousands of different personalities of themselves. And everybody Discovering What's in their mother's vaginas is why we got Syphilis Tuesdays. Without Syphilis Tuesdays, where would we be?

The Vibrator: That's a valid point About all the ears of The government listening & listening & listening... But how come You're All on fire? There's flames shooting out of your bodies!

The 10,000 clones: That's a lot of bullshit with a Spaghetti-of-words on top! And I always like to get on top, if anybody like to get down low. Because being on top is like Riding a dolphin into the fires of hell! Being on top is like painting your house with murder!

The Vibrator: You never get down low in the down low?

The 10,000 clones: Hell naw! I ain't like that!

The Vibrator: So if you like the down low, what about the up high?

The 10,000 clones: The up high is lots of sPaCe-aLieN-dRuGs! And lots of sPaCe-aLieN-dRuGs is so Penis without a penis! It's so Menstrual-fluid-sex with apples & oranges!

The Vibrator: It's so Menstrual-fluid-sex? But what about the Fleas?

The 10,000 clones: The Fleas is all about the elephants bouncing around your room! And that's all about the Hundreds of Human cadavers in your basement. And now and then, Shakespeare exploding into pieces Happens! Sometimes even Death from Wild Shakespeare psychopaths with AK-47s!

Death always be happening! So you gotta kiss Death with lots of Humor! Kisses falling all over death!

The Vibrator: But sometimes one of your hallucinations can bite you. That happened to me when My entire imagination caught on fire. That ever happen to you?

The 10,000 clones: Yes, but only with Decapitated strangers Running around upstairs in my attic. It's so Big-as-an-ocean with hopelessness! Lots of solutions to all the Bullets-in-your-brains! Lots of Lice for all the Words crawling in your hair! Solutions - problems – it's all a bunch of anal sex! Unless the anal sex happens With lots of Herpes walking by. Then it's Churches of Anal Sex for all the Priests of Pornography.

The Vibrator: I always wondered about that Wacko wonder! That clarifies all the Wandering rivers in my head. What do you think about Carjackings by philosophy students?

The 10,000 clones: I think it's a bunch of axe murderers with philosophy degrees. They're all making the world beautiful for the strange hUmAn-mAchDown forInE-bEinGs that We are becoming! But other people think that it's a lot of Sex percolating Everywhere! Either way, Drive-by shootings between rival gangs of philosophy students happens! See you gotta be prepared with lots of ice cream! Unless you Have zits of wisdom on your face & buttocks! Then it's Rabies & Doctoral degrees in philosophy for everyone!

The Vibrator: I like to change the subject, if I may, what about the Genital warts growing on all the nuclear missiles? And how do you play Yippee-Daba-do with a Mickey Mouse cartoon character that has a 10 inch penis?

The 10,000 clones: That's all about the Public toilets of Heaven! You got lots of Freaky adjectives out there in the Orgies of heaven! So be ready for the Vaginas that Percolate with lots of coffee! But don't worry about the Penises that will rise up to conquer the heavens! And My-Bonging-Blapping-penis always be falling down! And Glory-hallelujah-my-penis always be rising Up! You see the People throwing their sexual organs at each other? This kind of Behavior is so merry-go-round of lust! But that disentangles people from all the Testicles-wandering-around! Because of all the sPacE-aLieN-thOuGhtS wandering around the Universe!

The Vibrator: But that still doesn't answer the question about the Lost vagina of Cleopatra of Egypt. Or do you think that Jimmy Hoffa stole it?

The 10,000 clones: It's time for some artillery & explosions & stuff! Everybody sick and tired of Being happy! Everybody Wants Rocketships in their public toilets! And nobody Wants little lollipops as penises! Even the dogs & cats be Writing fairytales of Wandering fantasies!

The Vibrator: Really? Even the dogs & cats? But what about the Equator running around the world?

The 10,000 clones: The Equator running around the world be Fantasizing about Riding those rocketships outta here! But

I am not sure about the Monkeys of Mars. The Monkeys are one Partying group of Space aliens! And then those lions & tigers always be Playing with the monkeys' penises! And flying monkey penises always be bothering them baboons, so you gotta Castrate yourself! Unless there is a decapitated chicken around to save you!

The Vibrator: A decapitated chicken to save you from what?

The 10,000 clones: To save you from Volcanoes of Laughter! What else you need a decapitated chicken for?

The Vibrator: Is that why you brought a decapitated chicken with you today?

The 10,000 clones: Yeah! We're going to eat it!

The Vibrator: Cool!

The 10,000 clones: Let's smoke some weed first!

The Vibrator: You got some?

The 10,000 clones: Hell yeah!

177

What To Do With an Oversexed Tangerine

A man interviews the sheep he's fucking

The man: So what you be Hallucinating now?

The sheep: I'm Hallucinating about cars & buses & trucks clogging my arteries! I'm Hallucinating about The Grinch that stole my Sanity! I'm Hallucinating about Circus clowns in my soup!

The man: But the Soup of human brains tastes delicious! Why aren't you happy with Being a thought in a writer's brain?

The sheep: I'm nuts about Dinosaurs eating me! I'm nuts about Pulling out my penis on a city bus and announcing my candidacy for mayor of the city! And I'm nuts about dOgGy tEsTicLeS & mOrE doGgY teStiCleS & mOre dOgGy tEsTicLes!

The man: Why Steal everybody's penis? Look at all the Skies crashing everywhere! You like that Pyromania in a bottle?

The sheep: It's all Big hairy vaginas that taste like Summer! That's why I'm sad about All this sunshine! And I'm sad about Breathing with so much normality Around me! And I'm sad about dOgGy tEsTicLeS & mOrE doGgY teStiCleS & mOre dOgGy tEsTicLes!

The man: Sad about dOgGy tEsTicLeS & mOrE doGgY teStiCleS & mOre dOgGy tEsTicLes? But Look at me! So, isn't this

The deranged sunshine you've been looking for?

The sheep: I'm going to explode! Too much Thoughts from other people stabbing me! Too much Eyeballs upon my skin! And too much Fire in everybody's eyes!

The man: Too much Fire in everybody's eyes? How could that be? Lots of Crashing world is everywhere, don't you think so?

The sheep: I don't think! I do think! I think about Jumping out of my brains! I think about Sailing away into Some song that Drifts me away from here! And I think about Riding a donkey away into The Old Testament!

The man: You think about Riding a donkey into the Old Testament? But isn't that Lots of fire and lots of Laughter and lots of Leprechauns?

The sheep: Everything & everybody is Somersaulting everywhere! Everything & everybody is angry about All the rUmbLinG-ruMbLiNg-rUmBliNg! Springtime is charging at us once again! I'm angry about Those Birds singing those insults to us all day long! Frostbite! – Suicide! – Impressionism!

The man: Are you Happy about the buildings & streets crawling all over the landscape? Or are you Happy about the lAuGhiNg-bArKinG-dOgs everywhere mocking you?

The sheep: What isn't there to be Happy about? Everything is Happy with gangrene! And when everything isn't Falling out of our heads, then everything is Jumping into our heads! And when everything Around us is jumping up into musical notes, then everything is Screaming alcohol at you! It's hopeless!

The man: What's Hopeless? Are the spiraling-spiraling-spiraling words hopeless? Or is the Hungry page hopeless?

The sheep: It's all hopeless! Pages hungry for words is hopeless! 365 days trampling all over you is hopeless! And this unfulfilled storm of lust is hopeless!

The man: Your unfulfilled storm of lust is hopeless? But what about the Monsters of Happiness? And what about All the wars rampaging at you?

The sheep: I'm going to Let myself be eaten by bOuNciNg-haLLoWeEn-pUmPkiNs! And then I'm going to Drink all of the Darkness ! And then I'm going to Land in a totally different Book!

The man: Why would you do all that, when the Architecture is pissing exotic words all over you?

The sheep: Because of Weird buildings getting weirder every day, and the Floods of weirdness makes me want to Wet my pants! And Wetting my pants makes me want to Paint everything bright colors! And the Bright colors in my imagination makes me want to Eat the reader!

The man: But you should be happy! You should be happy with People jumping out of high-rise windows! And you should be happy with Orangutans blasting off to The future! And you should be happy with All the Death! So why aren't you happy?

The sheep: What's there to be happy about?! There's too much talking orifices in my Daydreams! And there's too much Silence in my Life! And there's too much People in my brains! Down with happiness! I'm against happiness! I never want to be happy ever ever ever ever again!

The man: Okay, suit yourself!

The sheep: Bye, and fuck you, and fuck your mother!

A Subway Rat Interviews You While You Wait for the Train

A subway rat: So, what's wrong with you? Why are you so happy?

You: I'm so happy because My bonkers is so Yellow! I'm so happy because My Alaska is so Mexican! I'm so happy because Fried rat is so delicious!

The subway rat: Well, you sure are happy! Tell us, just how happy are you?

You: I'm as happy as a hooker who has lost her vagina! I'm as happy as a madman who has found his madness! And I'm as happy as a nuclear war that

has lost its nuclear missiles! Happy! –
Happy! – Happy!

The subway rat: But happy is so insane-
asylum-gothic these days! How do you
feel about that?

You: I feel so happy, that I don't give a
fuck about The upcoming nuclear war!
I'm so deliriously happy, that all the
Artificial Intelligence devouring humanity
don't mean shit to me! All this
happiness! Happy! Happy! Happy!
Happiness like subway stations full of
murderous goblins! Happiness like city
buses floating up into an angel's
imagination!

The rat: But why are you happy if
mAniC-sPaCe-titS are everywhere? And
why are you happy if all the politics is
Going herpes?

You: Who gives a shit about all that Glorious incest?! I just feel myself smiling like Thousands of mirrors! I'm smiling from The bubonic plague to The aurora borealis! I'm so happy, that even my butt is smiling!

The rat: Your butt is smiling? What is your butt smiling about?

You: My butt is smiling about all the Weather balloons in the sky! And my butt is smiling about all the Clouds in the sky! And all the spermatozoa in my Balzac are smiling too!

The rat: Even your spermatozoa are smiling? But why are your spermatozoa smiling if Charles Manson just died?

You: My spermatozoa don't give a fuck about nothing, except going swimming up some lady's cunt! I was talking to my spermatozoa this morning! And my spermatozoa told me that they're happy! My spermatozoa told me that they're so happy, because of all the aurora Borealis! My spermatozoa are the happiest spermatozoa in all the world!

The rat: But what about the space aliens rioting in outer space? You don't think their spermatozoa are happier?

You: No way man! My spermatozoa are happier than trains cRaShiNg-iNtO-eaCh-oTheR! My spermatozoa are Wondrous with happiness! I have such happy happy happy happy happy happy happy spermatozoa!

The rat: Can I taste your spermatozoa then?

You: Yeah, sure, you wanna give me a blow job right now?

The rat: Yeah, I'd love to give you a blow job! Let's end this interview right now...

How to Grow a Farm of Penises

An interview with a butterfly

The reader: Yippee! Lots of yippee! You yippee with Motorcycle frenzy?

The butterfly: Yeah man! Everything yippee with So much motorcycle frenzy that I'm cumming in my pants! I gotta Shout with all the yippee! Sometimes, yippee be so Tender. You gotta Be so tomorrow with all that yippee!

The reader: So, tomorrow? You gonna Cum all over leprechauns with all that tomorrow?

The butterfly: Tomorrow be so hello & heaven with so much Penis rhythms! You know? Because Penis rhythms and Peanut-butter-rhythms and Disco-genocide-rhythms! I'm so tomorrow with all these rhythms! All that tomorrow be dancing with the yippee! And all the yippee be dancing with so much tomorrow!

The reader: Yeah, but I lost my penis in that machine! So, how Do I get my penis back?

The butterfly: Jumping-happiness-colors, and so much sky! Fluorescent-hamburger-jolly tonight! We gonna dance like flying buildings! We going to do flying buildings with all the yippee! We going to yippee so much Genocide! Lots of heaven with our wet dreams! You dig? You dig that Genocide?

The reader: Yeah, I dig that genocide! I also dig the Genocide with lots of caviar

& champagne! You dig the Cocaine all the way to Flying around the solar system?

The butterfly: You gotta fuck that English! You gotta do so much yippee to that English, that cum-is-dripping-from-all-the-English! Even now, These rotting brains of mine is so rhythms! So rhythms and so rhythms and so rhythms! Even the grasshoppers be so Incestuous! So touch the weather! Pee on the farm animals! Be lots of open arms with all the Naked words frolicking everywhere! Be lots of Strawberries with all the open legs! Immaculate conception for all the grasshoppers!

The reader: Immaculate conception for all the grasshoppers? But how's that going to impact all the yippie?

The butterfly: Fucking Goddammit to all the Lions & Tigers fucking in my coffee! Fucking Goddammit to all the verbs & nouns slithering & slithering At my feet! And fucking goddammit to all the Prostitutes parachuting out of the sky! I'm going to dance with a lot of fucking goddammit! I'm going to eat fucking goddammit until my stomach is crazy with space aliens! That's right! You gotta believe in a human eyeball at the end of your fork!

The reader: I believe in fucking God dammit too! So what's the future for fucking God dammit?

The butterfly: You gotta dance that fucking god dammit until The Dawn is leering at you! Too much tomorrow to believe in that fucking goddammit! But even with all the fucking Goddammit, lots of Capitalist politicians can happen! So you have to have eyes in the trees! You have to have ears in your ass! You have to have your nose Smelling everything across the Earth! And when your hands be masturbating the East with the West, well then, fucking god dammit!

The reader: But how the rhythms of Your hand & your penis going to Write this symphony? And how the fucking goddammit gonna do the Mermaids swimming around your apartment?

The butterfly: I'm so frustrated! Too much fucking god dammit everywhere! And I'm trying to create these BLAM-BLAM-BLAM rhythms! I'm trying to pick my nose with lots of Sexual excitement! I'm trying to scratch my hemorrhoids with so much Patriotism! We gotta have more diarrhea in our capitalist political speeches! You know what I mean?

The reader: Everyone wants more diarrhea in their capitalist political speeches! But, we have to find more tunnels to disappear into! Or do you disagree?

The butterfly: I agree with that, except when I disagree with that! And I disagree with that, except when I agree with that!

The reader: But do you agree, or disagree?

The butterfly: That depends on the Size of the penis! Even tomorrow, lots of Penis happened! I'm so awake that I'm sleeping! I'm sleeping with lots of tomorrow! I'm sleeping with lots of Sexy blowup dolls on my bed! I'm hibernating in the clouds. I lost my mouth, but I gained 2000 heads. That's why I believe in buttocks!

The reader: Everybody believes in buttocks! Buttocks buttocks buttocks?

The butterfly: Lots of buttocks, too much buttocks, flying buttocks, purple polkadotted buttocks, I'm so Planet of Pluto! I'm so Planet of Pluto that I didn't wake up this morning! I still haven't woken up! This interview is a dream!

The reader: This interview is not a dream!

The butterfly: This interview is a dream! How else can you explain all the Flying airplanes in this room? And what about the walls full of bouncing-bouncing-Boobs? And how do you explain all the Zombies & ballerinas doing the Big-big-boom-boom here?

The reader: Well, if you're dreaming, then why don't we Change places? I'll become a butterfly, and you become a person?

The butterfly: Fantastic!

The reader: Let's go!

The butterfly: Okay.

How to Grow Lions & Tigers in Your Empty Stomach

A Pigeon interviews a naked man at a bus stop

A pigeon: So how's that liberal Overflowing toilet going? And how's the conservative Diarrhea-all-over-the-carpet going?

The naked man at the bus stop: Well the liberal Overflowing toilet is so Much in outer space! And the conservative Diarrhea-all-over-the-carpet is so God's testicles! So you have God's testicles running for President, and you have the Liberal Anus Monster running for

President. I like to Jack off to liberal Political speeches! And I also like to jack off to conservative Political speeches!

The pigeon: I see. So you're very bipartisan. And what about the liberal Smelly pussy, and the conservative Herpes on the penis?

The naked man: Well, it's like Herpes sprinkled all over your Beautiful family values. You sprinkle the liberal Herpes all over the capitalist Cock. And you sprinkle the conservative Herpes all over the capitalist Cock. It's all very Christmas with lots of Everywhere burning down...

The pigeon: But Santa Claus ejaculating Christmas all over my face is very Sexy feet! And that feminism and born-again Christian conservative stuff going S&M together?

The naked man: Yes! Yes! Yes! It's all a bunch of Liberal & conservative S&M, or maybe a bunch of Anal sex with the American flag pole, so much censorship! Censorship! Censorship! Censorship! And most of the time I have no idea whether I'm being censored by a liberal or a feminist or a conservative or a religious nut. The best I can do is just pee my Words all over the liberals & feminists & conservatives & religious nuts. They're all the same! They're all that same American flagpole up your butt!

The pigeon: So explain to us the difference between the liberal endless wars & the conservative endless wars.

The naked man: Well, first I scratch my iTchY-sWeaTy-sCrOtuM, then I See how all the Fish swimming through the buildings downtown be Smiling, and this

helps me to accomplish the nirvana of
Licking the yellow stains off of public
toilets, and then the Dalai Lama cums
And gives me all of his snot & boogers.
But, when you add the whorehouse full
of Statue of Liberty clones servicing the
corporate billionaires, and then the
Machines of Cock-a-doodle-doo go Oh-
Oh-Oh with the Pussycat, and now you
have a Winner!

The pigeon: But with the conservative
Five-dollar crack whores giving
Republican Party politics a Transvestite
Boner, and the liberal Cocksucking-in-
the-alleyway giving Democratic Party
politics a Nice warm hug, what you think
about the Big hairy crotch?

The naked man: You take the
Democratic liberal politics and you
Smoke some crack with it. And you can

always perform Fellatio with the Republican conservative politics. This is where black nationalism comes in. Because the black nationalists are always Performing fellatio & Cunnilingus on rich white liberals, that is when they're not licking-the-asses of the rich white liberals. As for the white supremacists, they're a bunch of Violent psychopaths. They're so dangerous!

The pigeon: I see the Buttocks of Polite liberal society Everywhere. But what about the white supremacists & the black nationalists licking ass together?

The naked man: Yes, that and a bunch of Snails squirming all over Uncle Sam's big black Dick. But not without the Mustard. And now for the Feminists & religious fanatics trying to whitewash sex out of everything. And, Of course, white supremacy is always worse than black nationalism, much much worse, but still both the white supremacy & black nationalism is a bunch of Overflowing Toiletism. It's a bunch of Wild toilets running amok!

The pigeon: And please tell us about the difference between a female president bombing the fuck out of other countries, and a male president bombing the fuck out of other countries.

The naked man: The difference is All about the syphilis & gonorrhea. And then there's female cops shooting a black man, instead of a male cop shooting a black man, which is all very Liberal-overflowing-toiletism. And don't forget the Midgets fucking in outer space!

The pigeon: And please tell us the difference between a female boss paying

you peanuts, and a male boss paying
you peanuts.

The naked man: Yes to Midgets fucking
in outer space! And the difference Has to
do with a delicious plate of scRaMbLeD-
hUmaN-bRaiNs. And with all of the
Zombies in your testicles, you are going
to have to read Shakespeare to all the
kangaroos hopping in New York City. And
that's why Penis love from a stranger in
the alleyway Is So Jesus Christ! You see?
You see that Urban fungus growing all
over your skin?

The pigeon: Now, if you could please
explain the difference between a
traditional "toxic" masculine heterosexual
four-star general Ordering the killing of
innocent civilians, and a transsexual
four-star general Ordering the killing of
innocent civilians.

The naked man: Well, the transsexual four-star general is more sexy to me, particularly if he has a nice ass! Because a Transsexual four-star general with a nice ass Really makes my erection Go cock-a-doodle-doo! I want to fuck transsexual four-star generals up the ass until The sex robots conquer the Earth! And while I'm fucking all the transsexual four-star generals up the ass I want Lots of SPLAT WHAM BOOM! And I want a big aquarium inside my head! And I want it now!

The pigeon: That doesn't seem very progressive of you. If you want to fuck the transsexual four-star generals up the ass, should you want to fuck the traditional heterosexual "toxic masculine" generals up the ass as well?

The naked man: I want to fuck
everything up the ass! I want to fuck the
canon of English literature up the ass!
And I want to fuck French Impressionism
up the ass! And I want to fuck the Nobel
Prize for literature up the ass!

The pigeon: And what do you think of
affluent liberals gentrifying working class
neighborhoods?

The naked man: I think that affluent
liberals are a bunch of Hypocritical-toilet-
faces! And I think affluent conservatives
are a bunch of Crazier-than-thou! And
then there's sticking my finger up my
butthole! Sticking my finger in-&-out of
my butthole is Almost as good as sucking
the priest's cock! It's like Having a
vacation in Beethoven's brain! And it's
like Sunshine all over your private parts!

The pigeon: I also like to stick my finger up my butthole. Perhaps we could play some Church choir music while you stick your finger up your butthole, and I stick my finger up my butthole, and while we're all sticking our fingers up our buttholes, we can sing an opera of McDonald's hamburgers together.

The naked man: Sounds great! Let's do it!

Ping-Ponging Boobs Bouncing Down the Street

A catfish Frying in the pan interviews a hungry man

The catfish: So you Fish in space alien brains for Around-the-world? Or You Prefer to castrate your own penis?

The hungry man: I be turning like A delicious pig on a rotisserie! I jump out of the pig's butt and now I'm a human! I become So many naughty adjectives when I go out sinning! I go sideways sometimes. I'm like a sideways Marquis de Sade with lots of Mayonnaise! So much jumping! Jumping like Vibrators in the crotch of the Queen of England!

The catfish: Why Eat other people's babies, when you can eat your own babies?

The hungry man: I'm as sick as goldfish swimming around inside Satan's testicles! My brains be Growing with universes of Sexual fetishes! I have a feverish Waterfall-of-words to give! My head turns around & around! I want so many new heads!

The catfish: Why is that? Is all this Gobbledygook of boiling solar systems going gazooks?

The hungry man: Beastiality & oversexed Martians & Church choirs of cocaine! So much Centuries of herpes behind me! So I whirl around! But then, I am conquered by herpes monsters! Meanwhile, all the buildings are sick! The sky has a fever! The windows are drooling everywhere!

The catfish: Yes, but Hookers be throwing their neon vaginas at Santa Claus. And then again, SPLAT goes the Big Vagina! What do you say to that Washington DC Of seXuaLLy-tRanSmiTTeD-diSeaSeS?

The hungry man: It's all going Zonka-Zonka-Zonka in a 360° angle of Pleasure! So, I can't find a sidewalk for my feet. So much imaginary worlds in the way! The ground runs away from me! There's no more sky above my head! The city suddenly disappears, and then reappears, and then Ka-BOOM goes the Herpes!

The catfish: And then Ka-BOOM goes the Herpes? But this is Your entire world burning down, no?

The hungry man: It's so much no that it's a yes! So much yes that it's dizzy! Everything dizzy with Endless-swirling-faces-around-me! I tried to keep my feet on the ground, but outer space grabbed me and took me away! And then The sky hits me with a Big Vagina! It's too much hurricane inside of me!

The catfish: But all the hurricanes inside of us are So sweet. And that's why All the families across the nation are slicing each other up with knives. Yes?

The hungry man: I can't Penis with that kind of Symbolism! The words keep jumping out of my hands! How can I use words when they won't stand still?! These words never stand still! With so many words hopping about, you're bound to trip on one of them! I try to Kidnap 300 million people, but then I'm surrounded by so many Screaming words, that I have to Take a shit in front of City Hall! I keep finding myself walking through the Sahara desert, even though I'm walking down the streets of Manhattan. How can this Big-venereal-disease-of-happiness Be happening? I have to Find a new anus to talk to. Or else Lots of incorrect grammar with drive-by shootings is bound to happen!

The catfish: But if Growing-human-heads happens, then it'll be Siamese twins! And then everything will be all right with Siamese twins for breakfast! Yes? Yes with a Sexually transmitted disease for me?

The hungry man: Lots of yeses to all the
Sexually transmitted diseases! You've
got yeses running around & around you.
So you've got to Walk with all the
sideways lurking about. You know what
I'm Jewish? Because when there's so
much up-and-down hiding 5 minutes
away, then banana peel!

The catfish: But that's too much banana
peel! And then there's the Giant
construction crane that keeps growing
out of my head. What say you to that?

The hungry man: It's like a solar system
kicking you in the ass! It's like elephants
trampling through your space station!
Even if you're eating pieces of the moon.
That's why you start peeing Blue & Red &
green everywhere! And all the doo doo
on the sidewalks speaking Elizabethan
English up to you. So, you've got to have

ears like Trees! Otherwise you won't hear all the Paintings! Lots of buildings slipping everywhere! You've got to have some side-to side. Side-to-side is just so Mass shooting with your every day. And your every day isn't Happening anymore. That's why vomit! Lots & lots of vomit! Add some Baroque-rococo to your vomit. Absolutely delicious! Delicious with Crashing helicopters! So eat your own vomit! Because soon you won't have a head!

The catfish: Won't have a head? But if that happens, then Endless-barking-dogs will be jumping out of everybody's butts! And what Nights full of Crack-whore-mermaids will be where then?

The hungry man: All the where be doing lots of whats! And all the whats will be allergic to the whens lurking about.

Because when you have lots of when lurking about, then all of the whats get afraid! They're afraid of a Sky full of giant lemons & oranges!

The catfish: And what about the adjectives? Are they part of the conspiracy?

The hungry man: You have to swallow the adjectives! If you don't swallow the adjectives then time will Eat you! And we will be lost without time!

The catfish: Oh no! Time has disappeared!

Monsters All Night Long!

A Drunken man interviews a mouse

A drunken man: What? You want Giant silence?

The mouse: Yes! Because of penises! Because of vaginas! So much penis & Vagina to parade through all your fantasies! We love a long night drifting across the centuries! And the long night loves us! So we strive for the flowing floods of creativity! The volcanoes & storms & lightning of the mind is so so soooo! That's the babbling disharmony of our brains going around & around!

The drunken man: That's the Babbling disharmony of our brains? But pUbiC-hAiR-ciViLiZaTioNs are Very intellectual! Isn't that Lots of farms growing Marijuana up?

The mouse: Yes all the time! So much yes that Murderers write poetry with the blood of their victims! So I'm painting lots of Death in bright red everywhere, but My dog is painting lots of eVeRyThiNg-faLLing-dOwn, and now Smelly panties! Smelly panties is up up up! So up up up that The Temples of Smelly Panties are falling! And that's So sideways with Sexy secretaries!

The drunken man: But! Siamese cats! Genital warts! Do you love my feet?

The mouse: Loving your feet is like Sodomizing Jesus Christ! That's why everybody has foot fetish! Everybody

having foot fetish is Patriotic! Patriotic
with lots of Grenades exploding! And so
much Grenades exploding is why we
Peanut butter ourselves.

The drunken man: And that so seXy-
sMeLLy-pAnTieS! Puppies jumping into
our mouths! Isn't that Up with so much
Sunny day?

The mouse: It's down with a bunch of
sHaKeSpeAreaN-gAnG-bAnGeRs, is what
it is! And that's why I love you! And I
hate you because of The emptiness all
over the walls! And I love you because of
rivers of graffiti art spreading
everywhere! The penis trees of
Christmas! The Genital-wart-hamburgers
of Zebras! It makes you wonder about
The zombies of Washington DC.

The drunken man: I'm wondering about
The zombies of Wall Street. Are you

wondering about The zombies of Wall
Street?

The mouse: I holler! I stamp my feet
onto the ground! I shoot my eyes at
everybody! So what I'm really wondering
about, is The insanity of the normal
people! The insanity of the normal
people is so Ejaculating all over the
public toilet floor and leaving it there for
the next person to see! And that's why
I'm having French Impressionist
erections all the time! So much heart
attacks! Heart attacks with Doggy
fucking! Heart attacks with licking &
licking that sweet kangaroo vagina! And
I –

The drunken man: Have you had heart
attacks with Happy?

The mouse: That's a Round-and-around
question! It's the kind of question that

causes Motorcycles to zoom off to All the answers. I'm so Exploding into Thousands of pussys! Screwdriver! Screwdriver! Screwdriver!

The drunken man: The screwdrivers of Anger?

The mouse: Lots of blow me! Blow jobs for the kangaroos! Blow jobs for the Penguins! So much blow jobs for An eternity of cocaine! We really Have reached the Himalayas Of Mars with all these blue jobs!

The drunken man: I hear blow jobs are even running for President! And I wonder –

The mouse: Wonder about the blue oozing down the canvas! Wonder about Puppies wagging their tails as they wait in line to be eaten by me! That's why I strive for The pubic hairs of Santa Claus! Striving and striving and striving for lots of Pubic hairs growing out of my books! My hands grab all of the Feces in all of the toilets of the world! My brains try to Create a giant toilet the size of the universe! My eyes try to see God's buttocks on a sunny day! I try to Eat myself! I need a sledgehammer! I need a sledgehammer to accomplish Poetry! I need a sledgehammer to destroy all Reality! I will build My imagination with a wrecking ball!

The drunken man: Wrecking ball is so Big penis feminism! Wrecking ball and wrecking ball and wrecking ball?

The mouse: I build the past with Sticking my big penis in feminism! I piss Christianity all over the future! I'm trying to accomplish the Grand fellatio of Jesus

Christ on the cross! I'm trying to build the Greatest biggest monument to the male penis in the world! I'm Devouring everything around me, and doing Anal sex to all the everything around me!

The drunken man: Everything! Everything! Everything!

(He dies.)

What is Murder Made Out of?

A pigeon interviews a homeless man

The pigeon: The sunshine is filling me with death! How do I Grow vaginas all over my flower garden?

The homeless man: It's the film! It's the film of Cannibals devouring vegetarians all night long! It's the opera! It's the opera of Domesticated animals singing in line at the slaughterhouse! It's the play! It's the play of Knives slashing through the audience! It's the painting! It's the painting of roosters with human heads eating nuclear missiles!

The pigeon: But what Lunatics will you be inviting to your cannibalistic dinner tonight? And what Poems will you read to your guests before you devour them?

The homeless man: This is a Festival of Neanderthals! This is drinking Springtime straight out of the Glass of Poison! We paint the film! The film is poetry! The poetry is a play made out of Words dripping with blood! We cut ourselves open, and we throw our blood on stage. This is the Heaven of Madmen! We be so outer space on drugs! Juvenile delinquents all of us! Even if we're old! We are senior citizen juvenile delinquents! Rampage! Vandalism! Public sex!

The pigeon: Public sex? Vandalism? What kind of rampage is this?

The homeless man: Rampage! Yes!
Toenails! Paintings of the impossible
splashing & dripping everywhere! Films
of Everything Impossible clashing with
reality! Onstage we Scream impossible
dialogues of impossible characters!
Onstage we Perform one genocide after
another! We perform the Greatest
obscenity on stage! It's Smelly! It's All
the foul words that make life so good!
You see the audience vomiting?

The pigeon: I see the audience vomiting,
And that's wonderful! But how Do you
turn the vomit of the audience into art?
In Which Smelly public toilets do you
perform your plays?

The homeless man: Blood all over our
bodies! Blood all over the ceiling! Semen
all over the audience! Do art with
murder! Do your murder with art! Do

your drive-by shootings with a touch of Picasso! Stab someone with lots of Renoir! That's what we need! We need hoodlumism in art! We need art dripping in blood!

The pigeon: How about art dripping in Life & death? And what are you tripping on?

The homeless man: I'm tripping on All the words boiling & boiling & boiling around me! I'm tripping on The sun talking to me all day long! All of us be tripping on lots of Night words dripping off of everything around us! It makes our plays more Blasting off! Our films are about All the everything dancing around us! Our novels are about the cannibalism of everyday life! Our lives are so much prison cells and prison cells and prison cells! So it's bananas with All the politicians in the zoo! It's Latino rhythms with The Western Hemisphere sinking in blood! It's African rhythms with the chains of slavery! It's rock 'n' roll with Beethoven and more Beethoven and more Beethoven!

The pigeon: But how come Beethoven gets on stage and plays the electric guitar? And what's up with Your mouth always Creating chaos that makes everybody's ears Go into shock? You In another century again?

The homeless man: We all be Traveling back & forth between the centuries! That's the Hieroglyphics of it! We paint the pOrNogRaPhY all over the Art museum walls! We dance like iNsUrRecTioN out in the streets! With our hands we turn the streets into a workman's art gallery! With our eyes we create New visions of what the future should be! With our words we infest everything with a feisty-feisty-feisty! We are hoodlums! We are artists! We are writers! We are criminals!

The pigeon: Are you criminals of time travel? Or are you criminals of art & literature & comedy?

The homeless man: We're the criminals of Culture! We're culture criminals! We're the criminals of Sex! We're sex criminals! We're proud to be criminals! We piss all over the art galleries! We use the nation's most prestigious literary magazines as toilet paper! We riot and riot and riot!

The pigeon: You riot and riot and riot? Why?

The homeless man: We riot the riots of Rioting! We riot the riots of Revolution! We turn our art into riots! And we turn our riots into art! This government is doo-doo! We smear our own doo-doo all over Wall Street & Washington DC!

The pigeon: So it's painting revolution all over canvas after canvas! And what is the Hotdog of it all?

The homeless man: The Bourgeoisie are ignoramuses! They control everything, but they know nothing about art or literature! In fact, they care nothing about art or literature, but they want to control it! So the best thing to do is to pee all over the bourgeoisie!

The pigeon: So let's do it! Let's pee all over the bourgeoisie!

Let's go!

How to Impress a Blowup Doll on a Date

An interview with a man on death row

The reader: So what the fuck man?

The prisoner on death row: Fast Verbs charging everywhere! Everybody Parachute out of each other's buttholes now! Need so much Universe! So much Universe that you Eat all the homes on your block! WOW to the Insanity of endless time! Penguin penis so Out of this Bing-bong-flippy-flop! Tornadoes to everybody! Everybody dance like tornadoes! Now! Fish brains! Yes!

The reader: Why the yes if You fucked an alligator last night?

The prisoner: That's a medieval dungeon full of Sex dolls that come alive at midnight! So much why why why with that Artificial intelligence brains boiling out of your computer! We need more Shotguns pointed at the brains of artificial Intelligence! More Crocodiles to eat schoolchildren! Fish flying to other planets! Running off to Siberia in outer space! Your mother's pussy is the rocketships of desire! dEsiRe – deSirE – dEsiRe! I feel Like pulling out my penis here in public!

The reader: And I feel Like lowering my pants and mooning all the passerby right now. How about that? And how about the Words growing like dandelions everywhere?

The prisoner: You can't Discover The desert of The night without loneliness!

And you can Always burn down civilization with your books! Fire! Swift-rabbit-Rocketship! Beep! Beep! Beep! Torment! The torment of Eating another man's cum out of your wife's pussy! Make lots of civil war with torment! So much torment that Nothing matters but the taste of blood! Ravens! Crows! Storms!

The reader: Are you talking about the storms of Planets flying by? Or are you talking about Mass castration for Christmas? Is tOo-mAnY-eYeBaLLs here to stay?

The prisoner: My wife so sexy for other men is so many exclamation points that I want to masturbate! maStuRbaTe – mAstUrbAte – masTuRbAtE! East Village! Paris! Latin America! It's all Masturbating in the blender together! In the blender we throw all the Art & Pornography together! We must start up lots of new festivals for art & pornography!

The reader: But what are you going to do with all the new Festivals of art & pornography? Are you going to dooby-luby-booby it?

The prisoner: It? It! So much it! Grab all the it and tappa-dappa-zappa all that it! Female breasts growing out of your computer! The words are full of cancer! cAncEr – caNceR – cAnCeR! Dig into the cancerous society! Expose all! Expose all your Zinga-Zonga! Rip the curtains of hypocrisy away! Show high society (both liberal & conservative) for the hypocrites that they are! Sledgehammer! Sledgehammer to everything now! I want to jump on a motorcycle out of

here and out of everything!
Sledgehammer to the status quo!